Leap of Faith
By Melissa Tarantino

© 2016 Melissa Tarantino

All Rights Reserved

All rights reserved. No part of this book may be reproduced or transmitted in any form or by any means, electronic or mechanical, including photocopying, recording, or by any information storage and retrieval system, without written permission from the author, except for the use of brief quotations in a book review. For information address Missy Tarantino PO Box 12, Ault, CO 80610

All characters appearing in this work are fictitious. Any resemblance to real persons, living or dead, is purely coincidental.

http://wwwmissytarantino.com

2 Corinthians 5:7 For we walk by faith, not by sight.

Table of Contents

January Blues

Season of Love?

Leap Day

Let's Do This!

Car Woes

Office Space

Rose

Ace in the Hole

Vacation

What is Love?

Stage Fright

Surgery

December

Ice

Turning the Tables

January Blues

Some days it just doesn't pay to get out of bed.

That was how Mary Beth's week had gone. On Monday, her alarm failed to go off. On Tuesday, she broke a shoe walking into work. On Wednesday, her car refused to start. On Thursday, she got a speeding ticket. And on Friday, she managed to lock her keys in her car.

By Saturday, she was ready to stay in bed, head under the covers and shut out the world. *If I stay here*, she reasoned, *nothing can go wrong*.

Then her phone rang. At first, she ignored it, but every time it went to voicemail, whoever the annoying person was would call again. She sighed and struggled out of her comforter fortress. She pushed her messy hair out of her eyes and reached for it on her bedside table.

"I *knew* you were there!" came a loud, shrill voice, which bounced around and lodged inside Mary Beth's head. "Did you forget that we had a breakfast date today?"

"Yes," Mary Beth mumbled, "…..no….maybe?" Her brain slowly picked up another gear as she tried to register first of all who the tyrant was, and secondly, why they thought there was a date.

"It's Saturday!" came the much too cheerful voice again, still in high octave range. "What have we done every Saturday since, I don't know when?"

Mary Beth groaned as the fog inside her brain lifted and she realized who the voice on the other end belonged to. She pulled her legs over the edge of the bed. The floor seemed safe enough. Maybe nothing would go wrong today. "I'm coming, Angela." She croaked in her morning voice.

She dragged herself into the adjacent bathroom and blasted the hot water. Soon steam wafted around her and she stepped into the shower.

Half an hour later, hair still wet, Mary Beth walked out of her apartment building to find her best friend leaning against her car. Smiling, Angela hopped over to Mary Beth and put her arms around her, engulfing her in a giant-sized hug. Angela's purple down coat muffled Mary Beth's greeting.

As snow began to fall gently around the girls, they climbed into Angela's red Honda and drove to their favorite little café. Angela linked her arm through Mary Beth's and tugged her along to the door, which boasted of "The World's Best Cinnamon Roll". She acted as if she hadn't seen the shadows under Mary Beth's eyes or her down turned lips. She carried on, bantering about the weather and how pretty the snow looked until they reached their quiet table at the back of the café.

Taking off their winter coats, the girls sat down at the square table covered with a cheap red and white checked plastic cloth. As if on cue, both of them took a deep breath, drawing in the warm, comforting smells of cinnamon rolls, coffee, and bacon. The waitress came over with menus, which they waved away.

"I'll have some hot tea," Mary Beth started.

"And I'll have the coffee," Angela chimed in. "And we will split one of your cinnamon rolls."

Turning back to Mary Beth, Angela couldn't hold back any longer. "So, what gives? You aren't yourself lately. You could go on vacation with those bags under your eyes." She leaned forward with a concerned look.

Mary Beth lowered her head and began to pick at her cuticles. "It's nothing," she muttered, not daring to look at her best friend.

"Not buying what your selling, my dear," Angela said, crossing her arms and frowning. "I know a bad mood when I see one. This cloud hanging over your head is bigger than Eeyore's!"

"Everything seems to be going wrong in my life right now, is all," Mary Beth managed to say just as the waitress arrived with their decadent breakfast. The giant cinnamon roll was served on a dinner plate with a generous dollop of butter and a cup full of frosting.

Angela was silent while they each dug their forks into the soft, warm pastry. She had known Mary Beth since they were in middle school. She was like a sister, best friend, confidant and partner in crime, all rolled into one person. Seeing her friend so down was hard for her to take. Her mothering nature wanted so badly to hug the hurt away. But she knew that Mary Beth wouldn't want that. Mary Beth was as independent as they came. She didn't ask for help for anything. Angela remembered their first week at college. Mary Beth was so homesick she could hardly stand it, but she had refused to allow herself to call home to talk to her mom because she wanted to prove she could handle it on her own. Angela knew that Mary Beth would share when she was ready, so she filled her mouth with gooey, cinnamon-y goodness and waited.

After a few bites, Mary Beth broke the silence. She began to tell Angela about her week. "Monday morning started off with my alarm not working. Of course, I was late to work. My supervisor was waiting for me at my desk and he chewed me out royally. He acted like I do this every day, but you know me, if I'm on time I feel like I'm late! I managed to get back into his good graces by the end of the day by working through my lunch hour and staying late to finish up his copying. You should have seen me, I was such a suck up!" A small smile made its way across her face.

Angela laughed. "I can just picture it. 'Yes, sir. Right away, sir,'" she said in a sing song way, all the while batting her eyelashes.

"Pretty good impression!" Mary Beth said. "I wish that was all that happened this week. I could handle that! On Tuesday, I was extra careful to make sure that I was on time for work and I even dressed up a little – still trying to suck up, I guess. I wore my favorite pair of heels. Remember the ones we bought when we went to Sole Food Shoes the day before we graduated from college?"

Nodding her head, Angela replied, "I LOVE those shoes. I was so jealous that they didn't have them in my size."

"Well, you're invited to the funeral, then," Mary Beth grimaced. "I stepped in a crack outside the office and broke the heel off."

"No!" gasped Angela, looking suitably shocked, dismayed and sad. Cute shoes were as important to her as breathing.

"Yep, broke it clear off and fractured it in the process. No hope of taking it to the hospital for surgery. They are dead for sure. So much for making a good impression after my mess up on Monday. Luckily, I had a pair of flats in my bag for just such an emergency. Too bad they were the ugliest pair I own. I don't know if my boss noticed, but it sure made for a bad mood on my part." Mary Beth stopped to take another huge bite of gooey cinnamon roll. A moment of silence for the departed shoes seemed appropriate.

"Wednesday wasn't any better. Unlike your fancy new car, my old wreck has started acting its age. I got in and it refused to start. No matter how much I sweet talked, it refused to turn over. At one point, I swear it was laughing at me!" Mary Beth looked annoyed when Angela started snickering.

"Sorry. I can just picture your car doing that. You've had that pile of junk since high school." She reached over and patted Mary Beth's arm. "Did you get it to work?"

"Nope. Had to call my dad and suffer through the 'take better care of what you own' speech. He did give me a ride to work, though."

"Wow, you weren't kidding about your week, were you?" Angela asked, sipping her coffee.

"Just wait. It gets better," Mary Beth said, brandishing her fork.

"No way!"

"Yes way. Thursday I managed to get myself a big, fat speeding ticket. I swear they changed the speed limit sign over night. I always thought that it was 65 coming down Mulberry on the other side of the interstate, but it turns out its 55 until the bottom of the hill. The state patrolman seemed so pleased with himself when he handed it to me, too. I actually turned around and went back to make sure he was right. Yep, 55, big as life. I'm such an idiot!"

She scraped the last of the frosting off the plate and washed it down with a gulp of her cooled tea. The waitress brought the check and the girls put the exact change down, just like they did every Saturday.

"We need to go shoe shopping to help you get over your week," Angela decided.

"I'm not sure I can afford a new pair, since I have to pay off that ticket," Mary Beth sighed.

"We can at least go and LOOK at shoes."

"I guess, if you want to," Mary Beth agreed half-heartedly, as they put on their coats. "I'd really like to forget about this week. Oh, yeah, I didn't tell you yesterday's tragedy. I managed to lock my keys in my car. I swear, my parents are going to make me move back home if anything else happens to me."

"You poor thing!" Angela once again gave her friend another grizzly sized hug.

They left the restaurant and headed back to Angela's car. The drive to Fort Collins went by quickly and they soon found themselves on the main street. The car seemed to steer itself automatically to Sole Food Shoes. When the girls stepped inside, they turned and grinned at each other. *Retail therapy really works*, Mary Beth thought. *Maybe this will kick start a great week.*

Two hours and three pairs of shoes later, Angela dropped a much more enthusiastic Mary Beth off at her apartment.

Season of Love?

Mary Beth looked in the mirror and applied one more coat of mascara to her already made up eyes. She stood back and twirled. Not bad, she thought, admiring her new dress. It was a beautiful shade of blue. The bodice was fitted and it flared out at the hips, accentuating her curves. The doorbell rang. Mary Beth walked quickly to the door, butterflies floating around inside her.

Opening the door, the first thing she saw was a giant bouquet of deep red roses. It moved toward her, and between the petals she saw a pair of bright blue eyes and a shock of curly brown hair. "Happy Valentine's Day!" said the handsome man behind the flowers. As he came into the room, he grabbed Mary Beth around the waist with his free hand and hugged her.

Mary Beth blushed, still not used to all the attention. She looked her new boyfriend over approvingly. He was tall, broad shouldered and had a kind face. He wore dark jeans and cowboy boots and a button-down shirt. Every time Mary Beth looked at him, her face flushed and she couldn't stop smiling. Today was no different. She couldn't believe that someone like Cory would want to be with her. One night, she, Angela and a group of friends had gone to the Lincoln Center to see a play. During the intermission, they had mingled in the lobby with the other patrons, drinking wine. Cory had come up to their group and introduced himself. Mary Beth had immediately been drawn to his rugged good looks and charm. After the play, Cory was waiting in the lobby. He handed her his business card and asked if she would like to go to dinner sometime. It took her three days to work up the courage to call him, but after some coaching from Angela, she finally made a date. They had seen each other practically every day since then.

She took the flowers to the kitchen and put them in a vase. She put her nose into the blossoms and breathed in appreciatively. She took a small black box off the counter, straightened the bow and returned to the living room. "I got you a little something, too," she said shyly.

Cory took the box, removed the ribbon, and lifted the lid. Inside was a silver and black diving watch. "I love this, Mary Beth! Thank you, so much!" He grabbed her around the waist and lifted her up as he hugged her to his barrel chest. He kissed her before putting her gently on the ground. She giggled and blushed. Cory immediately took the watch out of the box and placed it on his wrist.

Mary Beth grabbed her coat and the two headed out. On the street, Mary Beth paused and looked up at the night sky as she put on her gloves. The crisp air seemed to make each star stand out more than usual, or maybe they were reflecting the stars in her eyes. Either way, they added to the romantic feel of the night. Cory took Mary Beth's arm and led her down the sidewalk to his parked car.

"Where are we going for dinner?" Mary Beth asked.

"Oh, just a little place I know you like," Cory teased, smiling with his eyes. "It's a surprise!"

Mary Beth settled into her seat as Cory pulled smoothly into traffic. She tried to imagine which of the amazing restaurants around town they were headed to. Maybe D'Angelo's. Italian food in a beautiful Victorian house. Or maybe Fondue Memories with its endless selection of scrumptious cheeses and decadent melted chocolate. Way expensive, but way worth it. Her brow furrowed when they turned onto the interstate. She couldn't imagine why on Earth they were headed out of town.

Twenty minutes later they arrived at the restaurant where they had had their first date: Provenance, in Greeley. This place hadn't even been on Mary Beth's radar. They had only eaten there that one time. A rustic looking place, it served the most expensive and best cuisine in the entire town. All the upper crust of society came here to celebrate anything and everything, or just because.

Mary Beth turned to Cory with a look of surprise on her face. "Wow! This is quite a surprise! This is where we had our first date, remember?"

Cory returned her look with one of his own. Eyes bright, cheeks flushed, excitement in his smile. "Of course, I remember. That's why I picked it for tonight. A special place for a special lady," he said with gruffness in his voice.

They walked in, checked their coats and were immediately seated in the intimate dining room at a table set with fine white linen and real taper candles; red, of course. There were rose petals strewn on the table. Crystal goblets reflected the gentle light. Mary Beth's eyes also shone in the beautiful setting. Cory pulled out her chair for her and then went around to the other side and sat down.

Mary Beth looked down at her lap and took a deep breath. This was a big night, to be sure. It was the first Valentine's Day she had ever had a boyfriend, much less gone to a fancy restaurant with, on such a romantic night.

"What's wrong," Cory asked, concerned.

"I'm...um...just...um.... feeling a little overwhelmed by all this," Mary Beth said in a small voice, waving her hand to include the whole room.

"You shouldn't be, you fit in here like it belongs to you. You are beautiful." He flashed a big smile at her.

"Thank you," Mary Beth said, looking down and smoothing her palms on the thick napkin in her lap.

A waiter, dressed all in black, arrived to take their orders. Cory and Mary Beth chatted about their day. It was easy for Mary Beth to lose herself in Cory's gaze. His eyes never left her face as she spoke about all the little details that made up her life.

The restaurant was beginning to fill up with other couples, some declaring their love for each other; others flaunting their pocketbook, trying to impress someone new.

Suddenly, Cory stiffened. He continued to look at Mary Beth, but now his smile seemed a little less genuine, a little more strained. He began glancing around the room, as if looking for someone, or something. Beads of sweat appeared on his upper lip and at his temples. He reached for his water glass and his hand was visibly shaking as he lifted it to his lips. One gulp, two, three. As he took the last one, he began to choke.

Mary Beth's eyes widened and she quickly stood and walked to Cory's side of the table. She patted his back and handed him a napkin. "Are you ok?" she asked quietly.

Coughing, Cory shook his head and stood up. People around them started to stare. Mary Beth looked around uncomfortably, unsure about what she should do.

"I'll be right back," Cory rasped between coughs. He maneuvered around the table and quickly exited the dining room, clutching the napkin to his mouth.

Mary Beth watched him go, then returned to her own seat. The onlookers returned to their own conversations, show over. Mary Beth took a small sip from her own glass and kept glancing over her shoulder toward the exit, waiting for Cory to return. Five minutes went by, ten minutes. Their meal arrived and Mary Beth became agitated.

She turned around in her chair and looked hard at the exit, as if willing Cory to appear. When he didn't, she stood up and walked to the doorway. The lobby was full of people, waiting for their tables. Mary Beth frantically looked around and didn't see Cory, or anyone like him. She found the bathrooms and, taking a deep breath, cracked open the men's room door an inch.

"Cory? Are you in there?" she called, tentatively. When she heard no response, she went back to the front desk.

"Do you happen to know where my date went?" she asked the maître 'de. "His name is Cory Black. He made the reservation for us. I can't find him."

"Yes, I did see him a few minutes ago, he was speaking with a young woman and I believe they walked out together," the tall man said, looking annoyed at being asked.

"He left the restaurant? Are you sure? Tall man, curly hair, blue eyes, black shirt, white stripes?" Mary Beth asked, not believing what the man said.

"Yes, he left with a tall blond woman wearing a black dress. Now, please excuse me." He dismissed her with a wave of his hand, as if she were an annoying fly.

Mary Beth began to hyperventilate as the realization that she had just been abandoned in a restaurant by her date began to sink in. The sounds of people talking around her began to fade as her vision narrowed and she began to feel light headed. She shook her head slowly and turned towards the door. As she pushed it open, the crisp winter night air slapped her in the face and brought the world back into focus. *There has to be a logical explanation for all of this*, she told herself. *This can't be what I think it is, this can't really be happening to me!*

Focusing on putting one foot in front of the other, she climbed the stairs from the garden level restaurant to the sidewalk. Hearing voices, she turned, and saw Cory. He was standing next to a white car, his hands clasping the upper arms of a blond woman in a black dress. She was in full song, waving her hands, her voice a shrill sound in the quiet night. Mary Beth was too far away to hear the words, but the intent was very clear. She heard Cory reply in his deep voice. The woman put her hands on either side of Cory's face and pulled him down to hers. As if in slow motion, their faces came together in a gentle, caressing kiss.

Mary Beth turned quickly to head back into the restaurant, but the heel of her shoe caught in a crack in the sidewalk. Snap! It gave way to the twisting pressure. With a loud squeal, Mary Beth fell forward onto the hard, cold cement. Her palms slapped the sidewalk, and she managed to stop her fall before hitting her head.

Cory and the woman to turned toward the sound. Cory blanched and extricated himself from the woman's grasp. He rushed over to Mary Beth's side and helped her to her feet. Once she was standing upright, she pushed him away. He stumbled backwards.

"Get away from me!" Mary Beth sobbed. She tried to move regally down the stairs and failed miserably in her broken shoe. She made it to the door before Cory caught up with her. He put his hand on the door and held it closed. He leaned close to her and said, "Mary Beth, please listen to me!"

Once again, she shoved at his shoulder. It was like pushing on a boulder and had about the same affect. Seeing the set of his jaw and the darkness of his eyes, she gave up trying to move him. Instead she turned and began pounding on the door to the restaurant. Someone inside opened it and she slipped inside, past the people waiting for their reservation, and ran to their table.

Looking at the candles, the flowers, the glasses, and now the beautifully plated food, Mary Beth suddenly grew very angry. She jerked her purse off the chair and limped to the front desk. "My coat, please," she said through gritted teeth. Cory was at her elbow by this time, whispering in her ear, glancing nervously around at the curious eyes looking their way.

"Mary Beth, wait. Listen to me!"

She continued to ignore him, trying to make space between them in the crowded room.

When his hands closed on her arms, the sight of him grasping the blonde's arms jumped in front of Mary Beth's eyes. She pulled herself away and through clenched teeth, said, "Don't touch me!" Clutching her coat, she fled the restaurant. Cory followed her. Outside, she paused, managing to smack Cory across the face with her coat as she swung it around to put it on. "Serves you right," she said.

Up on the sidewalk, the woman was now sitting in the car parked next to Cory's, with the engine running and the lights on. When she saw Cory, she flung open the door and jumped out. Hair flying, she stalked over to where Mary Beth and Cory were standing.

"Who is she?" the woman demanded.

"Who am *I*? Who are *you*?" Mary Beth countered, her voice rising.

"I'm his girlfriend!" the woman responded pointing a long, red-painted fingernail in Cory's direction.

"Really? I thought *I* was your girlfriend!" Mary Beth said turning to face Cory, sparks flying from her eyes.

Cory turned his head from one woman to the other like he was watching a tennis match. His mouth began opening and closing. Nothing came out.

Mary Beth was beginning to have tunnel vision again. She turned away from the other two and stumbled down the sidewalk, fumbling in her purse for her phone. Hearing footsteps behind her, she put out her hand and shook her head. The sound stopped.

"Mary Beth, please listen to me," Cory begged. Screeching tires and a flash of headlights interrupted him as the blonde woman raced by. Angry horn honking followed and faded as she tore out of the parking lot.

"NO!! You don't get to talk to me, ever again," Mary Beth managed to say as sobs closed her throat. She held the phone to her ear and listened to it ringing. Cory started walking toward her again, and again Mary Beth held out her hand toward him, palm out. "If you come one step closer, I will scream," she warned, her voice rising.

"Sir, ma'am, is everything alright?" the maître 'd came into sight, his breath showing in the cold air.

"He might be fine," Mary Beth said, "but I'm not!" She glared at Cory.

"Sir, you must come in and pay your bill," the older man insisted.

"Yes, go pay the bill, you two timing jerk!" Mary Beth growled. "That's the least you can do."

Cory reluctantly followed the man down the stairs into Provenance to take care of the check. Mary Beth turned her back on him and began to talk into her phone.

"Angela, can you please come to Greeley and get me? RIGHT NOW!" she cried. "Cory.... Cory....Cory....Oh, Angela, I need you! Please?" She started to break down and cry.

Leap Day

It was Saturday again. It had become Angela's habit to call Mary Beth several times a day to check on her. Mary Beth couldn't seem to shake herself out of the funk she was in after the heartbreaking experience she had gone through. Two days ago, though, Mary Beth had yelled at Angela to leave her alone. She had hung up on her, so Angela decided to give her some space. *Maybe I'm being too pushy,* she thought.

This morning the phone rang and rang, but to no avail. Mary Beth just wasn't picking up. Angela began to panic. What was wrong? This wasn't like Mary Beth. Sure, sometimes it took a while for her to answer, but this felt different, somehow. Grabbing her keys, she rushed over to Mary Beth's apartment.

Lightly at first, Angela knocked on the door. "Mary Beth, it's Angela. Open the door." She leaned her ear against the door and listened. Nothing. Closing her fist, she began banging harder and harder. Still nothing.

Finally, Angela knelt and dug through her purse for the key Mary Beth had given her. She had grudgingly taken it two years before when Mary Beth had insisted she have it. "For emergencies," Mary Beth had said. *Well,* thought Angela, *this is certainly an emergency.*

She inserted the key and turned the lock. Calling out to Mary Beth she opened the door. The living room looked as it always did, neat as a pin. The pillows were fluffed, the rug was vacuumed, the magazines on the coffee table were neatly stacked and in line with the edges of the table. Frowning, Angela called out, "Mary Beth? Where are you? It's Saturday! Did you forget about breakfast?"

There was no reply. Quickly Angela crossed the room and went down the hall. Mary Beth's bedroom door was closed. With her heart beating in her throat, Angela turned the knob and opened the door. Red dots were scattered everywhere; the floor, the nightstand, the bed covers. Some were even stuck in the drapes. Angela screamed. The scrunched-up comforter in the middle of Mary Beth's bed jumped at the sound. Seeing the movement, Angela crossed to the bed and climbed on. She grabbed the covers and started to pull, afraid of what she would find underneath. When she was finally able to dig inside and find the cave Mary Beth had made, she found a very disheveled mess. Mary Beth looked like a vagabond from a movie set. Her hair was greasy and matted and covered her face. Her clothes were wrinkled and sweaty. Her face was red, blotchy and shiny. The smell of her unwashed body made Angela rock back.

"Mary Beth!" Angela cried. "What is going on? I thought you were dead!" She started checking Mary Beth for wounds, but found no blood anywhere.

"I am dead," Mary Beth whimpered, "just go away!"

Instead of going away, Angela reached in and pulled Mary Beth into her signature bear hug. At first Mary Beth stiffened and resisted, but Angela hung on. Before long, Mary Beth relaxed and melted into Angela's arms. Her shoulders began to shake and tears began to flow. Soon she was sobbing so hard that the bed shook. Angela just sat there, being Mary Beth's life line, waiting for the storm to abate.

After 15 long minutes, the storm broke. The clouds thinned and the tears became fewer. Soon all that was left were jagged breathing and sniffles. At that point, Angela drew back just enough to look in Mary Beth's eyes. Neither girl said a word or let go. An unspoken message of compassion and understanding and acceptance passed between them. Their bond of love would weather this, and any other storm.

When it felt safe to talk again, Angela said, "Come with me." She stood up and took Mary Beth's hand and led her to the bathroom. More red spots here. Angela accidentally stepped on one and it crunched under her foot. Looking more closely, she realized that it wasn't blood, like she'd originally thought, but dried up rose petals that she was seeing. Turning on the water, Angela said, "You'll feel better after a hot shower." Mary Beth nodded obediently and began to undress.

Angela left the room and closed the door behind her. She stood still and listened. When she was satisfied that Mary Beth was doing as she was told, she turned her attention to the battlefield in front of her. First, she stripped the bed and gathered up all the dirty clothes she found on the floor. Then she found the vacuum and sucked up all the evidence from the ill-fated bouquet. By the time the water was turned off, the bed was made, the curtains opened and nothing was left to remind Mary Beth of the disaster she had lived in for the past few days.

Angela went into the living room to wait for Mary Beth. Soon she appeared, dressed in jeans and a sweater, hair still damp from the shower. Her skin color had returned to normal, but her eyes were still puffy and tired looking. Shyly, she looked at Angela and said, "Thank you."

Angela stood and crossed the room. She hugged her friend, gently this time, and replied, "You are so welcome. I'm sorry I didn't come sooner." After a moment, she asked, "Do you feel like going to breakfast, or should I make you something to eat here?"

Mary Beth took a deep breath and replied, "It's Saturday! What have we done every Saturday since, I don't know when?" She smiled a small smile and grabbed her coat.

Their usual table was waiting for them when they arrived at Café on Main. The familiar sights and smells of the little place further improved the girls' mood. Their favorite waitress, Sandy came over with their drinks. "Do you ladies want your usual?"

"Yes, please," they answered in unison. "Jinx, you owe me a coke!" The first signs of a smile played around Mary Beth's lips.

Not one to beat around the bush, Angela asked, "Do you want to talk about it?"

"Not really, but you are going to bug me about it until I do."

"True. So, start at the beginning, and don't leave anything out," Angela said, crossing her arms and leaning back. She put on her best stern face.

Taking a sip of her hot tea, Mary Beth began, slowly at first, then speaking quickly as if she couldn't wait to get it all out of her system.

"After I hung up on you on Wednesday, it felt like my whole world had ended. I couldn't breathe in my tiny space so I left. I got in my car and drove. I didn't care where I went, I just went. I wanted to get lost. I was crying and driving for at least an hour. I ended up at Horsetooth Reservoir. I pulled over and got out. I climbed up some rocks and just sat there for a while. It was real peaceful, you know. A great place to think. After I calmed down, I decided that I needed to confront that jerk once and for all, so I drove straight to his house. Big mistake.

"I parked in front of his house. I sat there for a while, trying to figure out exactly what I wanted to say to him. I had it all worked out, but then I lost my nerve. I was just about to leave when the front door opened and he came out. Of course, he saw me. I got out of the car. I should have just driven away. He stood there on his porch and made me walk all the way to him. He didn't even meet me half way. I stood there for a minute, thinking that maybe, just maybe, he would start the conversation and apologize for his behavior, and explain himself, but no, he didn't. The jerk didn't say anything. He just stood there with this look on his face, like I had some explaining to do.

"What a jerk!" Angela said. "You didn't owe him anything, much less an explanation of your behavior."

"I know, right? It made me mad. I told him how he was the first boyfriend I'd ever had and how much I cared for him and how perfect I thought he was. Then I told him how he had broken my heart that night when I realized that I didn't mean anything to him and that he had been lying to me the whole time. I told him what a big jerk he was and that I deserved better."

"What did he say?" Angela asked.

They paused their conversation as a giant cinnamon roll slid onto their table. Picking up her fork, Mary Beth took a huge bite. "I didn't realize how hungry I was!" She quickly chewed and swallowed and took another bite. "Man, this is good!"

"What did he say?" Angela asked again, sounding a little impatient.

"You won't believe this, but he didn't think he'd done anything wrong. He said, 'We never said we were being exclusive.'" Mary Beth said, making bunny ears with her fingers. "I couldn't believe it. He said, 'I am a man, we aren't married. I don't see the problem of sharing this with lots of women.' When he said that he had the audacity to puff out his chest and strike a pose."

"Seriously?!" Angela said, wiping icing off her lips. "He really thinks he's God's gift to women?"

"Right? I mean, really, he is good looking, but not THAT good looking," Mary Beth said. "At that point I turned around and ran to my car and drove away. I came home and, well, had a fit. You saw what I did to his roses."

"What I don't understand is how did you go from being that mad to being the mess I found this morning," Angela said gently. "You scared me. I've never seen you act like that before. I honestly thought you had hurt yourself, or worse."

Mary Beth ducked her head and tucked a strand of hair behind her ear. "I'm sorry about that." Tears started welling up in her eyes. She reached for her napkin and wiped them away. Squaring her shoulders, she took a deep breath. "That wasn't the end of the story."

"There's more?" Angela asked, eyes wide, not sure she wanted to hear this.

"In the middle of my ranting and raving, there was a knock on the door. I thought it was you, so I opened it. Cory was standing there."

"No!" Angela gasped.

"Yep, in the flesh. The dirt bag himself. I was so shocked I couldn't speak. He said, 'Hey, baby, we need to talk.' Like nothing had happened that morning! Then he walked into my apartment without being invited in, like he owned the place, like he owned me! He acted like nothing was wrong, like we'd just had a fight and needed to make up. He went over and sat on the couch and patted the cushion next to him, like I was a puppy and would obediently come. I didn't, though. You'd be proud of me. I just stood there with my arms crossed. This time I was determined to make him start the conversation. Pretty soon he did. He told me that the other woman was indeed his girlfriend and that they had been dating for two years. Two years! He claimed that things had been getting stale between them and that when we met he thought I was the most 'magical' person he'd ever met. That was his word, magical. Ugh! Makes my skin crawl." Mary Beth rolled her eyes and shuddered.

She signaled the waitress. "Could we please have another cinnamon roll?" The waitress raised her eyebrows. "Really," Mary Beth said. "I'm starving." Sandy turned and walked away shaking her head.

Angela looked incredulous. "Those things are the size of home plate!"

"I know," Mary Beth replied sheepishly, "but I haven't eaten in two days. Cut me a break, will ya?"

Diving into the new pastry, Mary Beth continued her story.

"I didn't say a word to Cory the whole time he was talking. I could tell it bugged him and that made me feel so good. He got up and started pacing the room. He went on and on about how he didn't do anything wrong, couldn't I see his side of the story, we were so good together as a couple, blah, blah, blah. It took him 15 minutes to get it all off his chest. I didn't move a muscle. I stood like a statue. Finally, he said, 'Say something! You are making me feel uncomfortable.' So, I did. I said, 'Get out.' I didn't yell, scream or cry. I was real calm about it. I simply pointed to the door. He took one look at my face, hung his head and left."

"Good for you," Angela said. "I don't know if I could have had that much composure. I would have wanted to hit him, scream, something!"

"I know, right? I think that I had gotten all that out of my system before he got there. I mean, look at my bedroom! I just felt empty at that point. I was so emotionally drained, I couldn't react. Really, I think it had a bigger impact on him than if I had yelled. That's what he had expected to happen and he was prepared for a fight. When he didn't get that from me, he didn't know what to do. I felt totally powerful in that moment. After he left, though, all kinds of emotions rushed in. I just knew that I would never have another boyfriend and would die all alone. All my insecurities surfaced at once." Mary Beth gulped down what was left of her tea.

"How do you feel now?" Angela asked. "You certainly have your appetite back." She looked pointedly at the half-eaten monster cinnamon roll.

Mary Beth actually giggled. "I guess I have," she replied. "I don't know how I feel, really. I'm still kind of numb from the whole experience. I'm not sure what to do now. I do know that I will never date again!"

Just then the waitress returned. "Do you girls need anything else?"

"Just a to-go box, please," Mary Beth said.

As she laid their ticket on the table, the waitress said, "Happy Leap Day, make it a good one!"

"What did she say?" Angela asked Mary Beth. Her eyes were wide, like she just heard the magic words to open Aladdin's cave.

"Happy Leap Day," Mary Beth repeated the waitress' words. "You know, happens once every four years... extra day in the calendar... I wish Cory would take a flying leap."

"That gives me a great idea!" Angela exclaimed.

"We're going to make Cory take a leap?" Mary Beth asked hopefully.

"No, YOU should take a leap," Angela said enthusiastically.

"Excuse me?" Mary Beth asked, pulling back. She couldn't believe what Angela had just said to her.

"No, not like that, not literally," Angela said hastily, waving her arms. "I mean take a leap of faith."

"I don't get it."

"Whenever I have a setback in my life, I always look for a way to offset it. You know, like the time when I got fired from my job. Don't you remember? That's when I started that new exercise/dance class. I decide to try something new, take my mind off of my troubles. You need a new hobby or something." Angela was talking faster now. "Since today is Leap Day, let's change it to Leap of Faith Day! The day Mary Beth changes the direction of her life and starts fresh. What do you think??" She was breathless with excitement.

"Oooookaaay," Mary Beth said. "How do I do that?"

"I don't know," Angela said. She paused and took a last sip of coffee. "Let's make a list of things you wished you could do and then pick one and just DO it!" She reached for her purse and scrounged up a pen and a small notebook.

"This isn't going to work," Mary Beth said. "My whole life sucks right now: jerk of a boyfriend, boring office job, tiny apartment, crappy car… I wish my entire life was different."

"Maybe it can be. You just have to trust God with it. Now, let's start that list. You don't like the size of your apartment, so you could move. You don't like your job, you could get a new one, you hate your car, you could buy a different one. What else is on your wish list?" Angela paused, pen poised above the paper.

"I want to travel more," Mary Beth said hesitantly. "Maybe I could go back to school?"

"Yes! Those are all great ideas. Oh, I just had a thought. If we came up with enough ideas, you could do a new one every month for the rest of the year! This reminds me of that book I read, <u>The Road to Happiness.</u> The author wanted to see if she could make herself happier, so she made a list of 12 different ways she thought would increase her happiness and she added a different one every month for an entire year." Angela was so excited she was bouncing in her chair. "This is going to be fun!"

"I don't know," Mary Beth said. "It sounds like a lot of work. I'm not sure I'm ready for any big changes right now. I really don't want to become your pet project."

"Are you kidding?" Angela said. "This is the PERFECT time to do this. It will work, trust me."

"Why don't YOU do it, then," Mary Beth challenged, looking a little irritated.

"Maybe I will," Angela replied. Then she continued, "I'll do it if you will. Life is too short to be boring, right? Trust me, this will be good for you."

"Let me think about it," Mary Beth said, standing up from the table and reaching for her coat and the to- go box.

Let's Do This!

The next night, Mary Beth went to dinner at her parent's house. It was a small, government built place made cute by the addition of a redwood porch across the front. It had been many colors during the years that Mary Beth grew up there, but currently it was a light gray with maroon trim.

As she climbed the steps, she could hear voices inside. Her older sister Melody was already there with her large brood of children. Suddenly the door flew open and Mary Beth found herself the target of a silly string war. As suddenly as it began, the attack was over and the children ran off to the backyard to find another unsuspecting victim.

After extricating herself from the pink and blue strands, Mary Beth entered the house. She made her way through the living room to the kitchen where she found her mother stirring beans on the stove.

"Hi, Momma," she said, giving her short, thin mother a squeeze around her shoulders. "Where's Dad?"

"He's in the backyard, manning the grill. We're having a cookout," her mother replied, kissing Mary Beth on the cheek. "I'm so glad you made it!"

"Mom, where are the tongs for the corn? Oh, hi, Mary Beth," said her tall, overly thin sister Melody, coming through the sliding doors from the patio.

"Hey, Mel," Mary Beth said.

Melody swept past her and took the tongs from their mother, turned and walked back outside without another word.

"What's up with her?" Mary Beth asked her mom.

"What do you mean, dear?" Mrs. Gates turned back to the stove and poured the beans into a serving bowl. "Here take these out to the picnic table for me, please."

Mary Beth rolled her eyes at the back of her mother's head. When it came to her mother, her older sister could do no wrong. She was the favorite child. Shaking her head, Mary Beth took the bowl of beans out the sliding doors and down the steps to the patio. There she found her dad flipping burgers on the charcoal grill. He refused to get a gas one because in his opinion, "Everything tastes better with a little smoke on it."

She set the beans down on the rustic picnic table and walked over to her dad. "Hey, Dad!" she said and wrapped her arms around his middle. Her head came just barely to his shoulder and he put one arm around her, the other one busy shuffling meat. "Mmmm. Smells delicious!"

"Everything tastes better with smoke on it, you know," he said in his deep baritone voice. "Looks like we're ready to eat. Grab that platter for me, will you?"

After corralling all the children, everyone took their seat on the long planks that made up the seating around the table. Bowing their heads everyone waited for Dad to say grace. "Amen!" they all said and started to dig in. Her parents knew how to feed an army and today was no disappointment. Burgers, hotdogs and corn on the cob came hot off the grill. Potato salad, beans and coleslaw sat in huge bowls across the table. Pitchers of lemonade and iced tea sparkled in the dappled sunlight streaming between the leaves of the huge cottonwood trees that shaded the yard. It looked like a scene from a Norman Rockwell painting.

After the feeding frenzy settled down, the conversation began to shift from compliments to the chef to what was going on in everyone's lives.

True to form, Melody dominated the conversation, talking about all the wonderful things that were happening in her children's lives, how smart they were, how athletic and how artistic. Blah, blah, blah. When she finally paused to take a breath, Mr. Gates turned to Mary Beth and asked, "So, what's new with you, pussycat?"

Mary Beth groaned inwardly at the musical reference. Her parents thought they were very clever with music lyrics and movie quotes. Her dad could have an entire conversation without saying anything original. It was his gift.

"Well, as a matter of fact, I am thinking about making some changes in my life," Mary Beth started.

"Oh, that's rich," Melody said. "I can't see you changing much more than your socks." She laughed, but none of the other adults joined her.

"No, really," Mary Beth insisted, "I am sick and tired of my life being so boring and lately I've had some big setbacks. I want some excitement in my life!" She looked to her parents, silently praying that they would be supportive.

"We're so sorry that Cory turned out to be such a dud," Mrs. Gates said, wiping beans off of the baby's face.

"You deserve to have a little excitement in your life," Mr. Gates said. "You're young. Live it up a little!"

Melody snorted, "Excitement! What could you possibly do for excitement. You never do anything. I think you are afraid of your own shadow! When I was your age I went to Europe. What could you possibly think is exciting?"

Mary Beth looked at her lap and started picking at her cuticles. *Same old Melody,* she thought, *can't let anyone else have the spotlight, even for a moment.*

Melody's second oldest child chose that moment to fall backwards off the bench into the soft grass. She started screaming and everyone rushed to her side. Mary Beth sighed. *Nothing changes in this family,* she thought, *I might as well be invisible.*

When order was restored and tears were abated with the help of a cherry popsicle, everyone returned to their seats to finish the meal. Conversation ebbed and flowed around current events and summer plans. No one said anything about Mary Beth's plans for her future.

Soon, the table was cleared and the food was put away. When the kitchen looked sparkling and fresh, Mary Beth headed out the door. Her parents hugged her, her sister ignored her and life was just as it had always been.

Climbing into her old, broken down Honda with the paint peeling off the hood, Mary Beth pulled out her cell phone and hit speed dial. "Angela," she said, when her friend picked up, "we are SO doing this leap of faith thing!"

"Dinner with your parents pushed you over the edge, huh?" Angela said.

"Yes, it did. Mostly it was Melody. I want to make her eat her words. 'What could you possibly do for excitement.'" Mary Beth's imitation of her sister was snarky and made Angela laugh. She'd been to enough dinners at the Gates' house to appreciate Mary Beth's predicament.

"Why don't you come over here and we will figure this out," she suggested.

"On my way," Mary Beth said.

By the time she arrived at her best friend's house, Mary Beth was beginning to feel better. Knowing that Angela understood where she was coming from and what her family was like made her feel like anything was possible, as long as Angela was by her side. The door opened as Mary Beth walked up the steps. Seeing the smile on Angela's face brought one to Mary Beth's. The girls embraced and went inside.

The interior of Angela's house was filled with antiques. It was her obsession. She often joked about how she felt like she had been born in the wrong century. Mary Beth teased her about living in a museum. The girls settled themselves into two beautiful wingback chairs in front of her fireplace and began to talk. Mary Beth related what had happened at her parents' house and Angela made the appropriate supportive sounds.

"I want to know more about this 'leap of faith' idea," Mary Beth said.

"Well," said Angela, "I've been giving it a lot of thought and I think it would be good for both of us. We need to get out of our ruts and take some chances with our lives. You know, follow our dreams, not just settle for what comes along."

"I think I'm ready for something like that," Mary Beth said, sitting forward. "I just don't know where to start. I'm not really that good at anything, except being other people's doormat. You, on the other hand are so talented. I could totally see you opening your own antique store! You practically live in one right now." She gestured around her, taking in the beautiful furniture, knickknacks and artwork.

Angela blushed. "Thanks, but don't sell yourself short. You are talented in your own right. Remember how you helped my mom fix up her basement when my grandmother moved in with her? You are a genius when it comes to organizing things."

"That may be true, I do have a touch of OCD in me," Mary Beth giggled, "but you can't make a living at it, can you?"

Angela shrugged. "Why not? There are all sorts of jobs out there that aren't your mainstream college majors. You DO have a business degree, after all. I'll bet if you Googled it, you'd find out more."

That night, Mary Beth sat in her tiny living room, thinking about what Angela had said. *I wonder if I really could make money as an organizer? No one would pay for something like that, would they?*

Curious, she grabbed her laptop, fired it up, and typed 'professional organizer' into the search engine. Within 2 seconds her answer was in front of her, in the form of over 10 million hits. "What?! You've got to be kidding me!" she said aloud to the empty room.

Next, she went to YouTube and tried the same query. She found almost 70,000 videos on the topic. She found a few that centered on 'how to become a professional organizer' and watched them with rapt attention. "I could do this!" she said excitedly.

"Leap of faith, here I come," she said, dialing her best friend. They spent the better part of an hour discussing the ins and outs of how Mary Beth could get clients, start a business and quit her current job.

The next day, Mary Beth took extra care in getting ready for work. She put on her favorite coral colored top, which showed off her beautiful brown skin, a flattering pencil skirt and one of the new pairs of shoes that Angela had helped her pick out. She stood in front of her mirror, putting on her makeup, while simultaneously rehearsing her speech to her boss. "Thank you for allowing me the pleasure of working for you this past year. However, an opportunity has come my way that I simply can't pass up. Please consider this my two-week notice."

It had been a long time since Mary Beth had felt this excited and nervous at the same time. She fidgeted with her buttons while she waited to see her boss. Walking into his office, Mary Beth almost lost her nerve. She took a deep breath and made her speech. Her boss actually looked relieved to accept Mary Beth's resignation letter. Not at all what Mary Beth had envisioned. She had pictured the scene where her boss asked her not to leave, while Mary Beth stood her ground. It was a little bit of a letdown to know her boss wasn't willing to fight to keep her there. *Maybe this is leap of faith is coming at just the right time*, she mused to herself. The day proceeded smoothly and soon Mary Beth was headed out the door.

She spent the evening looking at YouTube videos and taking notes on everything she learned. She found out that it didn't really take much to get started; just a computer, a phone, a business card, and transportation to client's locations. Clients. That was the hiccup in this little plan. Where was she supposed to find people who would let her come into their homes and organize their closets and kitchens and other messes???

Mary Beth called Angela to get ideas. Angela suggested that maybe her mom might know some people who would want some help. Before long, Mary Beth had a lead. A woman in Angela's mom's Bunco group was looking for some help with clearing the clutter from her kitchen table.

That job led to another and before she knew it, Mary Beth had to go buy an appointment calendar to keep track of all the people who called for her help. Her evenings after work were booked solid and she didn't have time to touch base with Angela until that Saturday when they met for their ritual cinnamon roll breakfast.

"So, tell me everything," Angela started the second the girls sat down at their customary red-checked table. "Are you finding any clients?"

"I have been SO busy, thanks to your mother and her Bunco friends," Mary Beth said happily. "I've even made up business cards. Here." She proudly handed Angela one of the brightly colored cards. Emblazoned across the top was the name of her new company: <u>Creative Organization by Mary Beth</u>. "What do you think?"

"I love the name you chose; it is perfect to describe what you do. The colors pop, too," Angela said. "I am so proud of you. You really are taking this leap of faith thing seriously."

"Well, there's no looking back now, that's for sure. I gave my two weeks' notice' at my job. My boss seemed happy to see me go. I have a feeling he wasn't that pleased with me lately. I haven't told my parents yet. I'm a little worried about what they are going to say." Mary Beth made a face, then took a giant bite of her breakfast.

Angela looked Mary Beth in the eye. "I know you love your parents and care about their opinion, but you are an adult and this is YOUR life we're talking about. You should make decisions that make sense for you, not for them. You deserve to be happy, and you haven't been for many months!"

Mary Beth's eyes got big. "Wow, that was quite the speech. I didn't know it affected you that way. Thanks for the support. You're right, I know. I just worry about the lecture I know is coming."

"Sorry to get so emotional on you," Angela said, "but I do care. Also, you inspire me." She clapped her hands together like a little girl. "I have news!"

"What! Tell me," Mary Beth said, leaning forward, wide-eyed.

"I have to show you," Angela said. "Are you finished eating?"

The girls finished quickly and left the restaurant. The weather was getting warmer and there were hints of green on the trees downtown. Instead of turning left towards where she had parked her car, Angela walked down the sidewalk in the opposite direction.

About four doors down from Café on Main, she stopped, turned and said, "Ta-da!" She held her arms out in her best Vanna White pose.

Mary Beth looked to where Angela was pointing. "What? I don't see anything." In front of them was a store front with a 'For Rent' sign in the window. Suddenly, it hit Mary Beth. "Are you kidding me? You are going to rent this building?"

"Yup," Angela nodded proudly. "Your leap of faith inspired me. I decided to open an antique store. This place is perfect!" The girls leaned in and cupped their faces to the glass. Inside the empty storefront, they could see hardwood floors and crown molding, but not much else.

Mary Beth turned and hugged her friend, hard. "I can't believe it! I am so proud of you! When do you move in?"

"I'm glad you asked that, because I'd like to hire you to help me organize the space next week. I sign papers on Monday," Angela told her.

"Of course, I'll help you! You know that! You don't have to hire me, though. I'll do it for free. It's the least I can do to pay you back for believing in me and supporting me through my down times."

"It's a deal," Angela said hugging Mary Beth back. "Looks like we have our work cut out for us."

Car Woes

"It's time to take another leap of faith," Mary Beth said through gritted teeth as she sat by the side of the road, waiting for the tow truck. She was white as a sheet and her hands were shaking. She had been driving to Cooper to meet Angela for breakfast when suddenly her car pulled to the right and started making an awful racket. She stopped the car quickly and got out. When she walked around to the passenger side of the car, she gasped out loud. The rear tire was lodged inside the fender well, but wasn't attached to the car anymore. *This can't be happening to me,* she thought. Leaning her head against the car, she started to cry. *I could have been killed! The car could have flipped over so easily. Thank you, God, for protecting me!* It took more than ten minutes for her heart to beat normally and her breathing to slow down. When her brain started to work normally, she called her dad.

He finally picked up the phone after what seemed like an eternity to Mary Beth. She told him what had happened, feeling tears pricking her eyes. He listened quietly until she had finished, and then said, "Honey, I'm so glad you are OK. I can't come help you, though. Your mother and I are down in Colorado Springs, visiting friends for the weekend. I'm sorry. Call the tow service and they'll take care of you. Keep me posted. We'll be home tomorrow night. I love you."

After calling the tow service, she dialed Angela's number. "I've got some good news, and some bad news," she said. "First of all, I'm OK. Can you come get me? I'm in the pile of junk I call a car on the side of the road on Highway 14." She filled her friend in on the unpleasant details and was reassured that Angela was on her way.

Angela arrived 10 minutes later, and after cussing and discussing the unfortunate circumstances, the girls settled in to wait for the tow truck.

"I need a new car," Mary Beth decided. "I've never bought one before. I've always had to survive on hand me downs from Melody. I guess this is my leap of faith for the month. Will you help me?"

"This is going to be a fun leap," Angela said. "Of course, I'll help. What are you thinking about getting? A Ferrari? A Lambo?" She giggled.

"I like your style. I wish I could afford those. But seriously, I have been thinking about this a lot, especially since this piece of junk has been so much trouble lately. I've always wanted to own a Mini Cooper. Do you think I can afford one?" Mary Beth looked at Angela hopefully.

"I don't see why not, doesn't hurt to ask."

Mary Beth pulled out her cell phone and looked up the number for Mini Land. As she spoke with the representative her eyes brightened and a smile crossed her face. After she hung up, she was actually bouncing in her seat. "Not only can I afford it, they think they want my clunker!" she exclaimed. "Can you take me there today?"

Just then the giant flatbed tow truck pulled up. It was hard to miss, not only for its size, but the cab was painted to look like the American flag. After a brief discussion with the driver, the girls watched him expertly load the car onto the back. They then followed him back up the highway and onto Interstate 25. Soon they pulled into the Mini dealership. The tow truck drove around the back to the service bays and dropped off the car. Mary Beth paid him and thanked him for his help. Then the girls went off in search of the rep Mary Beth had spoken to on the phone.

Walking toward the building the girls oohed and ahhed over all the cute cars. There were so many to choose from. Soon they found the front doors and entered the building. Inside they saw the latest models displayed on stages. There were also racks of accessories for the Minis. Mary Beth squeezed Angela's arm in excitement. Everything was just so cute, it even SMELLED cute.

Turning to the receptionist, Mary Beth asked for Rob, the man she had spoken to on the phone. After shaking hands with the girls, he took them back to the service bays so Mary Beth could show him her Honda. After walking around it twice, checking the mileage and under the hood, and starting it up, Rob went to consult with a mechanic. Mary Beth looked nervously at Angela, feeling her dream of a new Mini fading.

The mechanic came out and went through the same routine that the sales rep had, but seemed to take twice as long. Mary Beth clutched Angela's arm. The men held a short conversation and then Rob came over to where the girls were standing, watching. "Do you want the good news or the bad news?" he asked.

Looking at each other, Mary Beth said, "Good news?"

"Sure," Rob said straightening his red tie. "I think we can work with what you have here to get you a better vehicle. The bad news is that I don't think I can give you very much in trade for the Honda. In fact, it will probably only be about $300 or so." He grimaced as he said it.

"I thought so," Mary Beth said. "It's not in the best of shape."

"That's OK," the salesman said, smiling at Mary Beth, "I've seen worse, believe me. Let's go have some fun." He led the girls back to the front lot. "Do you want to look at the new models, or pre-owned ones?"

"Oh, I can't afford a brand new one," Mary Beth said. "Let's look at the older ones. I like that one." She was pointing to a black Mini with red stripes on the hood and red wheels. It had sponsor stickers on the doors.

Rob laughed and said, "That's certainly an eye catcher, but that one's not for sale. The owner's son races that one."

Mary Beth looked incredulous. "People RACE these?"

"Yes, they are quick, light, and turn easily. Wait until you get behind the wheel, you'll see."

He took them around to the side of the building and showed them several cars. They picked out a white one with a black top. Angela climbed into the back and Mary Beth sat in the passenger's seat. Rob got behind the wheel and drove off the lot.

"This is SO cute!" Mary Beth exclaimed. "I can't believe we're doing this!" Angela echoed her from the back. They admired the large circular speedometer in the center of the dashboard. The sun roof was opened and closed several times.

"Your turn," Rob said, pulling over to the side of the road. He got out and watched as Mary Beth skipped around the car. He smiled at her enthusiasm. He showed her how to adjust the seat height and then got in next to her. They drove around a few back roads before heading back to the dealership. "What do you think?" Rob asked.

"I think I'm in love," Mary Beth said. "Do you really think I can afford this?"

"Let's go in and talk numbers," Rob said in his most professional voice.

Angela joined in, "I'm sure you can work something out."

An hour later, the girls left the store. Mary Beth following Angela in her new car. She couldn't keep the grin off her face and kept taking deep breaths. She wiggled and danced down the road, giggling and shaking her head. *I didn't know a leap of faith could make me feel so good!*

Office Space

As the weeks rolled by, Mary Beth found herself happily swamped with clients, wanting her to help them organize their lives. She turned her dining room table into her office space, and the living room became storage for all the pieces and parts she accumulated to help her with her job.

One night, Angela came over to drop off some client information. The girls were surprised how they were able to overlap their businesses. Mary Beth would sometimes suggest pieces of furniture to her people that she had seen at Angela's antique store. Angela shared Mary Beth's business cards with everyone who stopped in to see her.

She knocked on the door and heard a muffled, "Come in!"

She opened the door and her eyes widened in disbelief. Large plastic storage bins were stacked three high in one corner. A huge pile of colored plastic hangers had taken over the couch. In the middle of the floor where previously Mary Beth's coffee table used to be was a large black and yellow portable toolbox.

After she looked around and couldn't find Mary Beth in the mess, she put her hands on her hips and said, "You know, I have a great friend who can help you with your organization challenges."

"Ha, ha," Mary Beth retorted, emerging from between the stacks, "very funny! It's fine, really. I know where everything is in this place. It's right at my fingertips."

Angela raised her eyebrows. "You can't possibly be your best in this space. We need to look for a new place for you."

"No, no, I don't. Not really." Mary Beth said, looking a little apprehensive. "This is fine."

"What's wrong? You have that look on your face, you know the one. You are closing yourself off to a possibility," Angela said.

"I don't want to move. I love this place. It's my first apartment. I felt like such an adult when I moved in here. There are so many memories," Mary Beth pouted.

"Okay, okay," Angela said, holding up her hands as if surrendering. "It was just an idea. Here's another one. What if you kept this place to LIVE in and we found you a DIFFERENT space to work out of?"

"That might be ok," Mary Beth admitted.

Angela said, "Let's see what we can find." She threaded her way to the dining room table and sat in front of Mary Beth's computer. She typed 'office space for rent in Fort Collins' into the search engine. She selected one of the first entries and up popped dozens of listings. "It looks like there might be something here that would work for you."

"I'll have to think about it. Maybe I should have a realtor help me look. I don't want to get stuck with something long term and then find out that it's not working," Mary Beth said, picking at her fingers like she always did when she was nervous or stressed.

"That's another way to go," Angela agreed. "But you aren't getting out of this. Time for a leap of faith!"

Mary Beth sighed. "I know you're right. This one's just a little more emotional. I need to be an adult about this. My business is growing. I should be excited about needing a bigger space and an official office! Change is scary!"

Angela nodded, and reached out to hug her friend before they both started crying. "This is a good thing, Mary Beth. I'm so proud of you and all you've accomplished. Think about how the year started. Look at where you are now. So much has happened and you are doing so well." She beamed at her best friend.

"My family isn't taking it too well, so I'm glad I have you for support." Mary Beth squared her shoulders and said, "First thing tomorrow I will contact a real estate person and see if I can get something more professional than this." She turned in a circle and really looked at how messy and cramped her apartment had become.

The next week was a whirlwind of clients and visits to properties around Ft. Collins. It seemed that Mary Beth had seen every single building in the entire city by Friday. She was able to rule out many that she saw as being too big or expensive. Once she committed to finding a place, though, she found that she really enjoyed it. It was fun to imagine herself in some of the places. A few were way too fancy for her taste and too expensive for her bank account.

She narrowed the search down to one in Old Town, one in a business park on Harmony and one on College Avenue. Saturday morning, she showed the choices to Angela at breakfast. They discussed the pros and cons of each one. They sat and debated for so long that their drinks grew cold and they completely forgot to eat. Angela was as excited as Mary Beth.

After they paid their check, Angela insisted that they go to her store. "I want to show you something," she said.

Angela unlocked the door and swung it open, letting Mary Beth enter first. Sitting in the middle of the room was a beautiful antique desk with a giant red bow sitting on it. "Surprise!" Angela yelled.

"For me?" Mary Beth gasped. She covered her mouth with her hands and stood, speechless, while Angela danced around her.

"Yes, it's for you, silly, for your new office," Angela said. "I found it last week and it made me think of you. I thought you'd like something special for your first professional space. You do like it, don't you?" She looked at Mary Beth, suddenly worried that she'd messed up.

"Like it? I LOVE it!" Mary Beth said, throwing her arms around Angela and engulfing her in a bear sized hug. "It's perfect!"

Mary Beth walked over to the old oak desk and ran her hands loving along its smooth surface. She walked all the way around it twice, studying its curves and the subtle carvings along the top edge. She sat down in the matching chair and opened and closed each drawer. She could picture herself meeting clients, answering phone calls and working on her computer at that desk. *How could Angela have picked such a perfect desk?* She thought to herself. *Thank you, Lord, for such a thoughtful friend.*

The girls left the desk and went back outside. They climbed into Mary Beth's Mini Cooper and went to Ft. Collins. Mary Beth wanted to show Angela the properties she was looking at renting. They spent the rest of the morning admiring each one. By lunch time Mary Beth had made her decision. It was a small office space located off of Harmony Road. There were large old cottonwood trees surrounding the building. Her space was two rooms on the ground floor. The front one was square, had a large window and looked out on a large green lawn. There were lots of Canada geese strolling around the grounds. The back room was a little larger, but didn't have any windows, perfect for her storage needs.

The following week, Mary Beth signed the lease with butterflies in her stomach. *This truly is a leap of faith*, she thought to herself. *God, I'm trusting your lead on this.* Clutching her new keys in her hand she walked confidently out the door of the realtor's office. She drove directly to her new office and went inside. She couldn't contain her excitement any more. She danced her way from one room to the other and back again. There was even an attempt at a moon walk. Finally, she lay down in the middle of the floor and made carpet angels. Standing up, she dialed Angela's number.

"Guess where I am?" she asked, giggling uncontrollably.

For an answer, Angela squealed. Both girls started jumping up and down.

Out of breath, Mary Beth stopped and tried to sound serious. "Now comes the real challenge. I have to rent a truck to move in here. I need to buy some shelves and probably some art work for the front room. Maybe even some chairs for clients."

"I can help you, when I close the shop. Maybe there are some pictures here that would work. You are welcome to them if you want," Angela said. "You can rent a truck here in town if you want."

Over the next several days, the office took shape. Mary Beth was pleased with the outcome. Her new desk sat proudly in the middle of the office and there was enough room for two beautiful antique chairs, on loan from Angela. The artwork was also from Angela's shop and made the room look cheerful and bright. Mary Beth was still in awe that this was all hers. She closed her eyes and opened them quickly. *Maybe this is all just a beautiful dream*, she thought. *Nope, it's still here!*

Her client list continued to grow as more people shared her talent with their friends and family. Even the other businesses in her building took notice and came to say hi. One tenant hired her to help organize a filing system.

Thanks, Lord, Mary Beth prayed, *for providing me with this office and the opportunities that have come my way lately. I'm sorry for ever doubting You and how much You care about me. I am learning so much about really trusting you and allowing you to lead the way. I want to continue to practice these leaps of faith.*

And with that, she took one more look around, turned out the lights, and quietly shut the door behind her.

Rose

    June is a busy month in Northern Colorado, weather-wise. It is unpredictable to say the least. One day it will be sunny and warm and perfect, and the next will have lightning, thunderstorms and hail. It is also tornado season.

    Mary Beth sagged in her desk chair in the air conditioning. It had been a long, trying day. Her latest client was an old woman, whose family had hired Mary Beth to help her clean up her house. The woman was a packrat, to put it mildly. Some would consider her a hoarder. Every room was filled with at least 50 years' worth of collecting. There were boxes stacked head high, and bags upon bags of clothes spilling out everywhere. It was difficult to find a level place to stand. There were books, magazines, fliers, mail, newspapers and memorabilia taking up every square inch of space.

    And this lady, Rose, was attached to everything. The need to hang onto everything, no matter how small or insignificant had been deeply instilled in her.

    Every approach that Mary Beth had tried, failed. Rose was stubborn and hard headed. The first day Mary Beth had gone to Rose's house had ended in disaster. In her mind, Mary Beth had pictured herself as the angel of mercy, come to save this poor soul from all her clutter. Nothing could prepare her for what she saw.

Upon opening the door, the first thing that Mary Beth noticed was the smell. A mixture of thrift store, garbage can and dirt wafted around her. The woman at the door had a look of stubborn defiance on her face that said she didn't want Mary Beth there. Rose's daughter came with her and introduced Mary Beth to Rose. She explained to her mother that everyone loved her and was concerned with her safety. She told Rose that Mary Beth had been hired to help her organize the house.

Mary Beth managed to get inside the house that first day and attempted to clean up the living room. She would try to clean up an area, and Rose would be right behind her, putting things back, or filling the empty space with new stuff. If Mary Beth suggested getting rid of a pile of old newspapers, Rose would have an argument about needing to read through them first. If Mary Beth asked about donating an item, Rose said she couldn't possibly part with it.

They both were getting frustrated; Rose was on the verge of tears and Mary Beth's jaw hurt from clenching. Finally, Mary Beth said, "Let's take a break for today and try again tomorrow." She smiled at the old woman. She did like her, but could feel her blood pressure rising. She decided that before she spoke sharply and said something she would regret, she would make her exit and regroup. Giving Rose a hug, she walked outside and took several deep breaths.

Back at the office, Mary Beth reflected and prayed, *Lord, I don't know what to do. I feel like this job is going nowhere, but I don't want to give up. Rose is unhappy, her kids are unhappy. I'm unhappy. There has to be a way to fix this.* She sat in silence for a few minutes, just breathing and listening for inspiration. Then she turned to her computer and typed 'how to help a hoarder organize' into Google.

There were many websites and advertisements to choose from. Mary Beth found one that looked promising. As she read through the blog she had found, she came across an interesting quote. "If you found a man in the desert dying of thirst, you wouldn't run up to him and offer him a hug and tell him everything would be OK. You'd give him water! You have to fix physical needs with physical solutions. Emotional problems need emotional solutions, and spiritual problems need spiritual solutions. Hoarding often stems from emotional and spiritual issues that need to be addressed before a person can tackle their 'stuff'." Mary Beth sat forward. *This is just what I needed! I need to help Rose figure out why she can't part with her material goods, then maybe she'll be able to let go of some things. I've never done anything like this. Leap of faith, here I come.*

The next day, Mary Beth went over to Rose's house with a new outlook on the situation and a new game plan. When Rose answered the door, she had a wary look on her face. Mary Beth smiled and gave her a big hug. "Let's come outside for a little bit, Rose," she said.

Rose looked Mary Beth up and down for a minute, then stepped outside hesitantly. She followed Mary Beth into the yard and took a seat next to her on the park bench that was nestled in the shade under the huge cottonwood tree next to the house. She sat stiffly, hands in her lap. She felt a trick coming. She began rubbing her hands nervously up and down her legs.

Mary Beth gently covered Rose's hands with her own. "It's OK, Rose. I just want to talk. We've never really gotten to know each other."

"What...what...what do you mean?" Rose asked. She furrowed her brow as she looked at Mary Beth.

"I mean, tell me about yourself. What do you like to do for fun? What is your favorite color? What do you like to eat?"

Rose sat still, looking into Mary Beth's eyes, still waiting for a trick. Mary Beth looked back at her, patiently waiting for a response. Finally, Rose sighed. She only saw a person who genuinely was interested in her as a human being. Tentatively she said, "I love the colors of spring, when everything is fresh and new after the deadness of winter. I enjoy putting together puzzles and reading mysteries. I love lasagna, just like Garfield." This last comment brought a small smile to her lips.

Mary Beth smiled in return. "My favorite color is royal purple. I love Italian food, too. I really like to go for hikes up at Rocky Mountain National Park."

Slowly, Rose relaxed. Mary Beth continued to ask questions and listened as Rose told her about herself. She began opening up and the two women spent the next hour chatting about their lives, their families and their favorite authors. It became an easy conversation and the time passed quickly. They discovered that they had a lot in common.

"Would you like a glass of lemonade?" Rose asked Mary Beth.

Mary Beth nodded. "You know, that sounds very refreshing right now. It's starting to get really warm out here." They walked arm in arm to the house and went to the kitchen to prepare the drinks together.

Looking around the kitchen, Rose said, "Why are you being so nice to me today? I know that yesterday you were very frustrated with me." Her voice was low and full of caution.

Mary Beth took a deep breath and waded into the inevitable conversation. "Last night I knew you were very upset and frustrated at what I was trying to do for you and your family. So was I. I didn't know what to do to make it better. I spent a lot of time praying about it. I felt I should do some research on situations like yours and I learned that 'stuff' isn't the issue here. It's a symptom. I think that there is something deeper going on with you, something inside. An emotional reason that you have felt you need all these items around you. Am I right?"

"You prayed...about me?" Rose asked incredulously. "That was sweet of you. But, why? You don't know me."

"Yes," Mary Beth answered, "I did. I wanted to do the right thing by you. I feel like everyone has your best interest in mind, but they have left you out of the conversation. No one asked you how you feel about this, or me, or anything. Am I right?"

Rose found a kitchen chair and sat down. A tear trickled down her cheek. She wiped it away and looked at Mary Beth. "You are an amazing young woman, Mary Beth. You don't know what this means to me. You are right. I felt defensive yesterday. I know my daughter and her family love me and want the best for me. They have been hounding me for a long time about my...collecting. I have felt very lonely for a long time, probably since my husband passed."

"I read last night that there is sometimes an emotional cause to 'over-collecting'. If we can figure that part out, the organizing will fall into place. I also learned that this process can take a long time, months even. Are you up for the journey? I'd like to help you if you will let me," Mary Beth told her.

"I really like you, Mary Beth. I would like to think that you mean what you say when you want to help me. I just don't think that I can do this," Rose shook her head slowly. "I've been like this for a long time. You can't teach an old dog new tricks."

"Don't think like that," Mary Beth said. "Are you happy the way you are, Rose? I don't think you are. All the stuff you surround yourself with can't love you. How about if we just say we'll try and see what happens? Take one baby step at a time. We can stop anytime you want to. I won't push you, I'm beside you all the way. What do you say to that? I would love to spend time with you and to get to know you better."

Rose stood and went slowly to the sink. She put down her glass and turned to Mary Beth. "I can do that. Try, I mean."

"That's all I ask," Mary Beth beamed, opening her arms. The two embraced. "Now all we need to do is decide where to start. I suggest we start with the room you spend the most time in."

Rose nodded. "That would be the living room. It's also the first room people see when they come in, so it will make the biggest impression on my children when they come over."

"OK," Mary Beth said. "Next question, what kind of music do you like to listen to?"

"What does that have to do with decluttering this place?"

"Well," Mary Beth said, "Something else I learned is to make cleaning fun. Listening to your favorite music can relax you and make the work seem less like work."

Rose grinned. "In that case I choose country. I grew up listening to it."

"You got it. Country it is," Mary Beth found Pandora on her smart phone and set it to play country. The two ladies walked to the living room together while listening to Carrie Underwood sing "So Small". They turned and looked at each other when they heard her singing about how easy it was to get lost inside a problem and feeling like you were disappearing.

Rose's eyes widened. "Wow, did you plan that?" Rose asked.

"Not at all, but it seems to be a sign, doesn't it," Mary Beth replied. She looked down and saw goosebumps on her arms.

Taking a deep breath, Rose nodded her head. "Let's do this."

"OK, trust me on this. Go stand in the middle of the room and look at me," Mary Beth said.

Rose walked the narrow path she had created and turned around. When she looked up, Mary Beth was holding her phone in front of her. Quickly she snapped a picture of Rose.

"What was that for? I don't want you to take my picture." Rose frowned, starting to regret her decision.

Mary Beth led Rose to the couch and the women sat down together. Mary Beth showed her the picture she had taken. "A tip I heard about clearing out clutter is that people who live with it are so used to it that they don't see the problem, it looks normal to them. Taking a picture of it lets you see it from an outsider's perspective. See what I mean?"

"Oh, my, I didn't realize it looked that bad!" She covered her mouth with her hand. "Those piles are higher than my head!"

"An added benefit is that now we have a 'before' picture to compare our progress," Mary Beth said. "Time for my next trick." She pretended to look in her sleeves, like a magician. "I am going to set the timer on my phone for 10 minutes. I want you to bring me 10 of your favorite things in this room and 10 things you could get rid of. Ready, go!"

Rose laughed and stood up. She looked around and began to gather items and place them in two piles on the couch next to Mary Beth. "This is like a treasure hunt!" Mary Beth counted down the time as Rose searched through the piles. Soon the timer went off and Rose returned to the couch. Mary Beth gently moved the items to the floor by her feet so Rose could sit down.

"Now, I want you to tell me about the items you put in the favorites pile," Mary Beth said, lifting the first piece and placing it in Rose's lap. It was a photo album.

Rose ran her hand lovingly over the cover. "This is full of my family's pictures," she said quietly. "My kids mean the world to me." They spent the next 10 minutes going through the pages. Mary Beth never once tried to rush Rose. More than once she felt tears prick her eyelids as Rose shared stories of her children.

They talked about each item in the pile, one by one. Rose became very talkative about some of them, but with others she had little to say. After these items were fully discussed and set aside, they tackled the ones Rose thought she could do without.

Mary Beth asked for an explanation of why it was OK to let these items go. Most of them were either pieces she had duplicates of, or things she realized she had no use for. Rose actually laughed aloud on a few items. "I have no idea what this even is!" Mary Beth had Rose sort these items into three categories: donate, recycle, and trash.

The rest of the day flew by. When Mary Beth left, she took the items Rose had decided to get rid of with her. There wasn't much of a dent in the living room clutter, but there was a very big smile on Rose's face.

The next day Mary Beth returned and the two women continued to slowly wade through the piles in the living room. By Friday, the piles had shrunk to waist height. Rose's spirits continued to rise and Mary Beth was happy that she was actually making a difference in someone's life. She had filled her car with donations every day and taken them to the Goodwill store. She was so proud of Rose. As she left that evening, she gave Rose the homework assignment to continue working with a timer and only 10 items at a time. She promised to return on Monday morning.

When Mary Beth next stepped into Rose's house, she gasped out loud. The living room was an actual living room. Instead of seeing piles and pathways, she saw a coffee table, a couch and two overstuffed chairs. There were end tables with lamps and even a doily or two. On the coffee table was a plate of cookies and two glasses of lemonade, condensation trickling down the sides. She turned, wordlessly, and hugged Rose. When they stepped back, both women had tears in their eyes.

"I'm so proud of you, Rose," Mary Beth said. She gave the frail lady a hug. "We need to take a picture of this." She had Rose stand by the fireplace and snapped a picture.

Rose smiled and wiped her eyes. "Come and sit down for a minute. We have a lot to talk about."

The women sat down and each took a cookie and a glass. Mary Beth turned to Rose and said, "I know I gave you homework, but wow! You get an A for sure!" She pulled up the before photo she had taken of Rose standing in the living room and showed it to her.

Rose beamed. "Mary Beth, my family has been after me for years to clean this place up. I've tried, believe me! But somehow, it never stuck. I just couldn't make it work. When you came over the first time, I felt so defeated, like I had let everyone down. Then you came back. I was feeling defensive, but you broke through my walls by seeing ME instead of my junk. You took the time to care about what I wanted and what was important to me. I felt honored and respected and valued for a change. I didn't feel like a burden or an annoyance for the first time in a long while. I realized that stuff can't take the place of people. My memories are not tied to the physical objects and that allowed me to be more objective. This is the result. I've come to feel peace with my past, my present, and am looking forward to my future. I'm not perfect, a long way from it, but it's a start." She smiled and squeezed Mary Beth's hand.

"Oh, Rose, that makes me so happy. I had prayed so hard to be able to find a way to help you. I'm on a journey, too, and now you are a part of that journey with me. Things haven't been going very well in my life lately and I've taken on a leap of faith challenge. You were my leap this month," Mary Beth said squeezing her hand back.

"I've never been called a 'leap of faith' before. I kind of like it! The living room looks great, but the rest of the house is still a disaster," Rose said. "Do you have any more tricks up your sleeves?"

"I think I might just have a trick or two," Mary Beth said, smiling. "Do you feel up to another challenge, or do you need to take a day off. You've worked so hard already this past week."

They stood and walked through the other rooms. Mary Beth gathered up the donate items that Rose had set aside and loaded them into her car.

"You're here, I'm here, so let's do it," Rose said.

Mary Beth reached into her back pocket and pulled out a small, black plastic square. It was a child's game. It consisted of a black square frame, three inches by three inches. Inside the frame were eight one inch square tiles, each with a number on it. The numbers were all mixed up and there was one empty square.

"What is that?" Rose asked, confused.

Mary Beth explained. "It's a game. The object of it is to reorganize the numbered squares by sliding the tiles around, using the empty space, until you have them in the right order. It can be quite fun."

"What does that have to do with cleaning my house?"

"Well," Mary Beth said. "If you have items you want to keep, but they aren't in the right spot, we create a staging area, an empty space, and reorganize your belongings until everything gets where it is supposed to be, just like the game!"

Rose shook her head. "Clever girl. It never feels like work when you are around."

The women worked the day away chatting and sharing stories until dinner time. Mary Beth looked around the cozy house and put her hands on her hips. "I think we've done enough for the day, don't you? My car is full of donations. It's a good thing tomorrow is your trash day, because we are running out of places to put the bags!"

Rose nodded in agreement. "I can't believe how a child's game turned into a clean house. We are almost finished with the kitchen. I found tools I didn't remember I had. AND I found my kitchen table. I haven't seen that in five years! Next time you are over we will have to use the ice cream machine you helped me unearth."

"I'll take you up on that deal," Mary Beth said, wiping her forehead. "This summer heat is getting to me. Ice cream sounds like just the ticket." She pulled out her smart phone and checked her calendar. "The next available day I have is Friday. Will you be OK to work by yourself until then? You can always call me if you get stuck."

"Let me check MY calendar," Rose replied, teasingly. She walked over to the kitchen wall where a newly installed calendar hung. "I will write it down. Friday, it is." She penciled in Mary Beth's name with a flourish.

Mary Beth left the house with a tired, but contented smile on her face. Rose was quickly becoming one of her favorite people. She couldn't wait to come back and see what she had accomplished. The promise of ice cream was appealing, too.

The rest of the week was filled with small jobs and paperwork. It went by slowly and Mary Beth found herself thinking constantly about Rose. In all the time she had spent at Rose's house, not one of her three children had stopped by to see her. None of her neighbors had come over, either. Mary Beth began to worry about her elderly friend. Mary Beth sensed that she didn't get very many visitors. She decided to ask Angela to come with her sometime.

Friday morning finally arrived and Mary Beth drove through the quiet of north Fort Collins. The trees were old and full and made a canopy over the streets. The yards were full of bright irises and day lilies. Mary Beth's windows were down to take advantage of the cool air. Turning the corner onto Rose's street, Mary Beth saw people milling on Rose's lawn and an ambulance parked in her driveway with its lights flashing. She pulled her car to the curb as close to the house as she could manage and ran.

Stopping the nearest person, she asked, breathlessly, "What's going on? Where's Rose?"

The gentleman looked down at Mary Beth's petite face and frowned. "You'd better talk to her daughter," he said, pointing to a tall, thin woman wearing a black skirt and suit jacket, talking on a cell phone.

Mary Beth ran over to her, recognizing her from the consultation she'd had before beginning this job. "Hi, Emily, remember me? I'm Mary Beth. You hired me to help your mom. What's going on? Where's Rose?"

Emily looked at her with dazed eyes. "Mom fell this morning. She was able to get to her phone and call me. I was on my way to work. I called 911 and they got here just a few minutes ago. They think she broke her hip."

"Oh, no!" exclaimed Mary Beth. "Is she going to be OK?"

Just then the door opened and the paramedics wheeled Rose out on a gurney. Emily rushed over to her side. Mary Beth just stood there, frozen in place, watching, as if seeing things on a movie screen. Soon the ambulance left, Emily following close behind in her car. The neighbors all wandered back to their homes. Mary Beth found herself all alone on the grass. Her gaze wandered to the front door, which was standing partially open. She walked over, intending to close and lock it, but instead found herself walking inside. The living room looked much the same as it did last week. The kitchen was neat and clean. The ice cream machine was sitting on the counter, ready for service. She opened the refrigerator. The cream and milk were front and center on the top shelf. Tears streamed down Mary Beth's cheeks. Emotions gripped here. *What if Rose dies? Who will I make ice cream with? Will her kids even miss her? Will her neighbors?*

Wiping her face with the back of her hand, Mary Beth walked down the hall towards the bedrooms. She and Rose hadn't started tackling them yet. In the first bedroom, Mary Beth found where Rose had fallen. Several boxes looked like they had been disturbed. Their contents were spilled out on the floor. She stooped and picked up a baseball. She peeked into one box. It seemed to be full of sports equipment and memorabilia. She gently put the ball back on the floor and backed out of the room. She felt strange being here without Rose.

She went back through the house, found Rose's house keys, shut and locked the door behind her. She called Rose's daughter, was sent straight to voice mail as she expected, and left a message saying that she had locked up and had Rose's keys at her office. She also asked for Emily to call her with details about Rose's condition.

Next, she called Angela. She needed her friend. Mary Beth felt shaken to her core. She hadn't been prepared for this. Angela and Mary Beth had spoken about Rose frequently and Angela felt like she knew her almost as much as Mary Beth did. The girls cried together and made arrangements to meet at the hospital when they got more news.

Ace in the Hole

"This is our last box, Rose," Mary Beth said, sighing. She sat on the floor next to the wheelchair and pushed the box toward the old woman. They had been working steadily all morning, cleaning and sorting their way through the bedrooms.

"I feel the same way, dear," Rose said, looking down fondly at Mary Beth's curly brown head. "This has certainly been a long ordeal. Thank you for being such a trooper."

"I think you are the trooper, Rose, wanting to continue with our project when you are still recovering from your fall. I still feel terrible that you were trying to do things on your own. I should have been there to help you. I could have prevented the accident," Mary Beth's sincere pain came through when she spoke. "How are you feeling?"

"I think I have just enough energy to finish that box before we go make some lunch," Rose said, reaching out her hands.

Mary Beth handed her the first item in the box. They had finally made it to Rose's bedroom. Both of the other bedrooms had been finished quickly, as they were filled mainly with items belonging to Rose's three children. Mary Beth had called them and had them come and collect their boxes. Mary Beth knew this room would not be easy for Rose because it still contained many of her late husband's belongings. Mary Beth had learned how to read Rose's body language and knew when to ask questions and when to let Rose silently process her feelings. Ever since that first day sitting on the couch, they had maintained their pattern: give each precious memory it's due, then make a decision about whether or not to keep it in the family.

Today would be Mary Beth's last day working for Rose and her family, and it was bittersweet. She would miss spending so much time with the older woman, who had become like a grandmother to her.

The doorbell rang. Mary Beth ran to get it, since Rose still had trouble maneuvering the wheelchair. When she opened the door, her heart did a flip flop. Standing on the porch was a police officer. He was young, handsome, and his uniform was clean and crisply ironed. His dark brown hair was closely cut and his face freshly shaven. He smiled at Mary Beth warmly.

"Can I help you, officer?" Mary Beth squeaked.

"I sure hope so," the man said. "Is Rose home?"

"Yes, I'll get her for you," Mary Beth replied, turning away, blushing. She started to walk away, leaving him standing on the porch. She turned back to the officer and said, "Would you like to come in?" She gestured to the couch.

"Sure," he said, stepping into the living room.

Mary Beth ran down the hall and quickly told Rose about the policeman at the door. Rose had Mary Beth push the chair to the living room. Mary Beth's heart was beating in her chest. *What could possibly be wrong? Why were the police coming to Rose's house? Isn't he so cute? Stop that!*

When they arrived, the officer was standing by the fireplace, studying the family pictures on the mantel. He turned around and his eyes rested on Rose.

"Grandma! How are you?" he said, coming over and wrapping his arms around her.

Rose returned the hug and smiled so big her eyes disappeared.

Mary Beth's jaw dropped.

"Mary Beth, I'd like you to meet my grandson, Adam. Adam, this young lady is Mary Beth. She's the one who helped me to turn this place back into a home," Rose spoke quickly, with a lilt in her voice. It was easy to see that she was proud of her grandson. She was holding his hand and stroking his arm.

Adam reached the hand that was not being held captive to Mary Beth. "Pleased to meet you, Mary Beth. My family is so happy that you have been here for Grandma. We've been very worried about her. You did a wonderful job helping to get rid of all the clutter she had hung onto."

Mary Beth shook his hand, barely having the presence of mind to close her mouth and quit gawking. Her speaking capabilities had deserted her for the time being. She kept looking from Rose to Adam and back again, expecting someone to say, "April Fools!" *Oh, yeah, it's not April!*

When her voice box started working again, Mary Beth remembered her manners. "Would you like something cold to drink?"

"Adam, we were just about to make lunch," Rose chimed in. "Would you join us? It would be just like a party!" She beamed up at Adam.

"Sure, Grandma, I'd love to," Adam replied. "I was just about to take my break anyway."

The three of them made their way to the now spacious kitchen and Mary Beth got busy taking food out of the refrigerator, while Adam made himself at home, opening cabinets and pulling out plates, silverware and glasses. When all the food was assembled on the kitchen table, Mary Beth and Adam pulled up chairs on the ends opposite each other, with Rose in the middle. She looked like the queen surrounded by her subjects.

Mary Beth began to reach for some fruit when Adam said, "Grandma, do you mind if I say grace?" She quickly pulled her hand back and blushed. She looked down to hide her red cheeks and put her hands in her lap.

"That would be lovely," Rose said.

Adam took her hand and reached for Mary Beth's. Startled, she quickly placed her hand in his and reached for Rose's other one. Adam's hand was rough and calloused, while Rose's was thin and delicate. The threesome bowed their heads and Adam said grace. It was short, but heartfelt. When it was over, Mary Beth was reluctant to take her hand out of Adam's. It had felt so warm and safe. She felt herself blushing again. *What is wrong with me!*

As the three began eating, Rose did most of the talking, which was fine with Mary Beth. She was afraid she'd start stuttering again, or choke on her food. She learned that Adam had graduated top of his class from the police academy and had been a patrol officer with the city of Fort Collins for the past 5 years. He had been assigned to Rose's neighborhood not long ago and stopped by to see her every chance he got.

Adam looked over at Mary Beth. He liked what he saw. She was a petite girl with pretty, curly hair. She blushed a lot, which Adam found endearing. Rose gushed about Mary Beth's abilities as an organizer and Adam liked that Mary Beth downplayed everything that Rose praised. He learned that she was single, which he also liked. He found himself trying to set her at ease, which wasn't easy, as she jumped every time his radio crackled and dispatch sent out a call. He wanted to ask for her number, but wasn't sure how to fit it into the conversation, especially since his grandmother had hardly taken a breath the entire time.

Forty-five minutes later, Adam reluctantly made his exit. He hugged his grandmother and promised to come back soon. Mary Beth shyly walked him to the door and held it open for him. Adam hooked his thumbs into his duty belt and turned towards her. "Thank you for taking such good care of Grandma," he said. "I can tell that you mean a lot to her and you are good for her."

"Oh, it's been my pleasure," Mary Beth said. "I have really enjoyed spending time with Rose these past few weeks. I'm sad that the project is finished."

"What do you mean?" Adam said, frowning slightly.

"Your family hired me to help Rose clean her house and we just finished the last box right before you got here," Rose answered. "I won't be coming back anymore. At least, not to work," she added, "but I hope she will let me come back to visit sometime."

"I think she would like that," Adam said. *And so would I,* he thought to himself.

Mary Beth smiled. And blushed again. *Why do I keep BLUSHING!?!* "It was very nice meeting you," she said, looking at her feet.

"It was nice to meet you, too, Mary Beth. I look forward to seeing you again," Adam said.

Mary Beth watched him walk down the sidewalk to his patrol car. He turned toward the house as he opened the door. Seeing her standing there, he waved. She quickly waved back and shut the door. *How could a man that I just met have such an effect on me?* I'm acting like a high school freshman! She returned to the kitchen and helped Rose clean up the lunch dishes. Rose was in a cheerful mood, but Mary Beth could tell that she was pretty tired from the hard work of the morning. She wheeled Rose to her bedroom and helped her lay down.

"Thank you for everything, Mary Beth," Rose said, looking into Mary Beth's blue eyes. "You are an angel for sticking with this stubborn old woman!" She smiled tiredly.

"I enjoyed every minute of it," Mary Beth said, looking at the frail old woman. "I'm so glad that you came into my life. I'm going to miss our walks down memory lane, now that we have finished with all your boxes."

Rose frowned. "That's right, we are finished. I hope that doesn't mean WE are finished." She looked hopefully at Mary Beth.

Mary Beth smiled. "I'm glad you feel that was. I was going to ask you the same thing. I'd love to come back and just chat over some of your fantastic lemonade. And you still owe me some of your homemade ice cream!"

"That's right!" Rose exclaimed. "I'd forgotten all about that! We didn't get to have any because I am such a klutz!"

"No, you're not," Mary Beth shook her head. "You just don't know when to stop and ask for help. Please promise me that you will call me if you ever decided to lift anything heavy. Or call Adam. I'm sure he'd be over in a heartbeat!" Mary Beth could picture Adam, muscles bulging beneath his shirt as he helped his frail grandmother lift boxes from a high shelf. It was a very pleasant image. "I'll call you next week and we can set up a date for that dessert. Right now, I think I should take my leave so that you can get some rest." She patted Rose's shoulder and pulled the hand crocheted afghan up around her.

Mary Beth quietly pulled the bedroom door shut behind her and collected her things. She looked around the tidy house proudly. *Thank you, God, for helping me to help Rose.* She pulled out her phone and scrolled to the picture she had taken at the beginning of the project. What a transformation. Now, not a single box was visible. The furniture was old, but in good condition. Rose's personal touches were everywhere, from the Precious Moments figurines on the knickknack shelves, to the photographs on the mantel, to the pictures on the walls.

Mary Beth's heart swelled with pride, knowing that her leap of faith had made a huge difference in the life of another human being. She had learned so much about herself on this journey as well.

The next day was Saturday. Mary Beth awoke to the sound of birds chirping outside her bedroom window. She stretched luxuriously and smiled at the ceiling. What a beautiful way to start the day. Sunbeams streamed through a crack in the curtains. She could hear the leaves on the cottonwood tree rustling with an early morning breeze.

By the time Angela arrived to go to breakfast, Mary Beth was showered, dressed, and had even applied some mascara. Her hair was pulled back in a ponytail and she was wearing her favorite pair of jean shorts and a tank top. The forecast had said the temperature would be in the high 90s.

Angela hugged Mary Beth and said, "What gives? You look different."

Mary Beth shrugged and locked the door. "I don't know what you mean. I look the same as I do every day."

"No, you don't. Something's up," Angela said, following Mary Beth down the stairs and out of the building. She stopped and tilted her head to the side. "Did you color your hair?"

"No."

"Did you go shopping without me?"

"No."

"Did you get your nails done without me?"

"NO!" Mary Beth repeated, exasperated. "Nothing's different. I'm starving. Can we stop playing 20 questions and go get breakfast?" She opened the door to her white Mini and got in.

Angela went around and climbed into the passenger seat. She buckled her seatbelt and said, "I'm going to figure this out if it takes all day."

"Alright, Nancy Drew, as long as I can eat a cinnamon roll while you do it."

The girls drove to Café on Main. Angela continued to pester Mary Beth the whole fifteen-minute drive.

"New makeup?"

"No."

"Did you go to one of those tanning booth places?"

"No!"

"Are you trying a new kind of lotion?"

"No!"

When they arrived at the restaurant, Sandy, the tall, thin, waitress came over to the table with their drinks and silverware. "What's up with you?" she asked looking at Mary Beth. "You look different today."

"I know, right?" Angela said, grinning. "I said the same thing!"

Mary Beth laughed and shook her head. "There's nothing different, I swear!"

Angela and Sandy looked at each other. "Not buying it, sister. Something's going on. You have this... this... glow about you today."

Sandy said, "I know that look. Did you meet someone?"

Mary Beth blushed and looked down at the table cloth.

"Bingo!" Angela shouted. The other patrons in the restaurant turned and looked at them. She lowered her voice and said, "That's it! You met a guy!"

Mary Beth squirmed in her seat. Sandy walked away laughing, high fiving Angela before she went to get their breakfast. Angela turned to Mary Beth and asked, "So, who is he? Do I know him? Where did you meet?"

Mary Beth grabbed her glass of water and took a big drink. *Was Angela right? Am I in such a good mood because of Adam?* The more she thought about it, the more she realized that Adam was the reason the sun was so bright, the air so clear, the birds so chirpy. *Chirpy? What does that even mean? Wow, I have it bad!*

Angela was studying Mary Beth's face. She had that 'I told you so' smile on her face. "Ok, enough internal monologue. Spill. I want details." She wiggled in her chair, getting comfortable for the story.

"I think you must be mistaken, my friend," Mary Beth said. "I have nothing to 'spill' as you say." She arched her eyebrows and tried to look disdainful. She only managed to look constipated. She broke down and giggled. "Ok, there is this guy."

"Of course there is, now get on with it. I want to know all about him. I haven't seen you look like this in months," Angela paused, remembering when Mary Beth had met Cory.

Mary Beth's expression changed, too. Her mind went back to the last time she had told Angela about meeting a guy. Come to think of it, they had been sitting in this exact same spot that time, too. She shuddered.

"Sorry," Angela said, reading Mary Beth's face. "I shouldn't have said that."

"That's Ok," Mary Beth reassured her best friend.

The girls paused to spread butter and icing on the huge cinnamon roll Sandy had brought them. They munched their way through several bites before either girl worked up the courage to talk more about guys.

"Is it Ok to ask about it?" Angela asked.

"Yes," Mary Beth said. "There's not much to tell. I just met him yesterday." She went on to give Angela what she had wanted, details. Just saying his name gave her butterflies in her stomach. Her smile came back and she relaxed. The thoughts of Cory faded into the background of her mind. Not gone, just fuzzy enough to be ignored.

She talked about meeting him at the door and thinking that something was wrong. She laughed about how much she had stuttered when she found out he was Rose's grandson. She talked about saying grace and holding his hand. Every last piece of that visit was imprinted in her mind in vivid color.

Angela sat through the whole story, making all the appropriate noises at all the right places. Finally, she asked, "Are you going to see him again?"

"I don't know. I hope so," Mary Beth said. "I want to, but I'm afraid to. I know I'll run into him sometime because I promised Rose I'd come visit. The job is over now, so I won't be over there as much."

"Afraid to? You crazy? He sounds perfect for you!" Angela exclaimed.

"Yes, afraid. Look at how my last attempt at dating went. I walked blindfolded into a shooting gallery. And guess what, I got shot. I pretty much laid my heart out on a chopping block and got it hacked to pieces. He was a saboteur who used rose petals as a weapon! Want another analogy?" Mary Beth was breathing hard and her fists were clenched.

"I know, I know," Angela said gently, laying her hand over Mary Beth's white knuckles. She paused and let Mary Beth calm down. The touch of her friend's hand helped bring Mary Beth back to reality. Her jaw relaxed and she flattened her palms on the table. Angela didn't move her hand until she was certain that Mary Beth was back in control of her emotions. "Cory was a wolf in sheep's clothing, for sure. You didn't deserve that."

"Darn right I didn't. I never want to go through that again. It still hurts to think about it," Mary Beth said. "He took my heart, crushed it, and stomped all over it. I can't believe there are people out there like that. I don't know if I'll ever be able to trust a guy again. I know Adam's cute and all, but I can't, I don't want to, I mean, what if he turns out just like Jerkface? I don't think I'll ever date again."

"Yes, you will," Angela said.

"No, I won't. I'm going to be a spinster. I'll die alone in a nursing home. You don't know how it feels, you have never been through this," Mary said. "You have a great life. Nothing ever goes wrong for you. Your boyfriend is loving, your family is loving, even your goldfish is loving." She crossed her arms and glared at Angela.

"You are so right. About not going through what you did, I mean. My life is far from perfect, though," Angela said. "I haven't always had a great guy in my life. I've had a few weeds in my garden, too. Just because they didn't have thorns, doesn't mean they were fun to dig out. My GOLDFISH is loving? I don't even HAVE a goldfish. You're nuts!"

"Ok, so I exaggerated," Mary said, finally giggling at herself, "but you know what I mean. Here I find this great guy and I'm afraid to get involved with him. Not that he's asked me out or anything, but if he ever did, I don't know if I could. I would be devastated to find out that he's just another jerk."

"How do you know that he's a jerk? Everything you've told me about him is wonderful."

"Exhibit A, your honor," Mary said, pretending there was someone sitting in the empty seat next to her, "Cory A. Wolf. Also known as Two-timing Boyfriend."

"Just because Cory was that way doesn't mean that every man is that way."

"Doesn't mean they aren't," Mary countered. "Burn me once, shame on you. Burn me twice, shame on me."

"Ok, Ok. Time to bring out my Ace in the hole," Angela said, crossing her arms. "Leap of faith."

"I knew you were going to say that," Mary Beth huffed. "That's not fair. This is hard. I don't want to get hurt again."

"What if he turns out to be the greatest thing that ever happened to you?" Angela wasn't giving up without a fight. She had seen the way Mary Beth looked when she talked about Adam. There was a spark there and she intended to do everything in her power to see that spark grow to a flame. "Just trust. I can tell that you like the guy. Can't you at least give him the benefit of the doubt for one date? He already has one thing in his favor."

"What's that?" Mary Beth asked.

"His grandma," Angela replied, laying down her winning poker hand.

"Good point," Mary Beth admitted. "She does think pretty highly of him, and I trust her opinion. Okay," She sighed. "I'll take a leap. But only for one date! If he asks me out!" She pointed her finger at Angela's cute button nose. "No promises!"

Angela laughed and put her hands up. "Okay! Okay! I'll take it!"

The girls finished eating and walked out into the sunshine. To Mary Beth, it seemed like it wasn't quite as good of a day as it had started out to be. She felt a slight sense of dread at what might happen if she saw Adam again. *Leap of faith, leap of* faith, she repeated to herself.

They headed over to Angela's store and spent the next several hours taking inventory, rearranging and marking antiques. Mary Beth's phone rang. On the screen was a picture of Rose with flour on her nose. Mary Beth had taken the picture one afternoon when Rose was teaching Mary Beth to make donuts. Happily, she pressed the accept button and said, "Well, hello, Rose. How are you?"

A deep baritone voice answered, "I'm fine, Mary Beth. How are you?"

"Who is this?" Mary Beth asked, a concerned look on her face.

"Hi, Mary Beth. It's Adam. Sorry to confuse you. I'm at Grandma's house and she told me to call you on her phone."

"Oh," Mary said, mouthing *It's HIM*! and pointing to the phone dramatically.

Angela's eyes got huge. *What does he want?* She mouthed back.

Mary shrugged and carried the phone into the other room. "Is Rose OK?" she asked.

"Grandma's fine. She just beat me handily at a game of dominoes. She was bragging about you. Are your ears burning?" Adam replied, chuckling. "She wanted me to call and invite you over for lunch next week. What day works for you?"

"Oh, I don't know. I'll have to check my schedule. I don't have it with me right now. Can I call her back on Monday? I'm not near my office, I'm at my friend's antique shop in Cooper," Mary Beth said.

"Ok, I'll tell her." There was a long pause, then, "Um... How are you today?" Adam sounded uncomfortable.

"I'm doing fine. How are you?" Mary Beth replied. She wandered around the room, touching things, moving things, trying to figure out where this conversation was going.

"I'm…uh…fine. Uh…just…relaxing…" Adam paused and took a deep breath. "The truth is, Mary Beth, I wanted to call you but didn't have your number. I came to see Grandma and she suggested I call you on her phone. I couldn't stop thinking about you yesterday and wanted to see you again." He stopped and held his breath.

Mary Beth just about dropped the phone. Her hands were shaking. She looked around frantically for somewhere to sit before her knees gave out. Finding an old oak office chair, she plopped down. She didn't know what to say. *God, what do I do? I'm scared.*

She heard herself say, "That would be fun. What are you thinking?" *What am I doing???*

"I was thinking about maybe a picnic at City Park," Adam said slowly, sensing that Mary Beth might not be on board.

"Oh, ok," Mary Beth said, breathing a sigh of relief. *I could do a picnic. Wide open space, easy escape, public place.*

"Grandma wants to come, too, if that's ok. Here she is, she wants to talk to you," Adam said. He handed the phone over to Rose.

"Hello, dear," Rose said. "I hope we didn't call at a bad time. I was thinking about how wonderful the weather is and a picnic sounded so nice."

Mary Beth smiled at the sound of Rose's voice. The tension eased out of her body. *If Rose is with us, it's not really a date.* "No, this isn't a bad time. I'm just helping Angela with some antiques. I'd love to go on a picnic with you." Suddenly an inspiration hit her. "Would it be Ok if she came with us with her boyfriend? She's been missing you, too."

"Of course, dear, the more the merrier," Rose said. "Shall we say next Saturday at noon?"

Mary Beth nodded. "That sounds perfect. We'll see you then." She hung up and ran to the other room.

Angela looked up expectantly. "What happened?"

"You have a date next Saturday," Mary Beth said, smiling.

"Huh? I don't need a boyfriend, remember? I already have one."

"Well, technically, it's a double date, but there's going to be five of us," Mary Beth said, adding to Angela's confusion.

"You are making no sense, whatsoever. Start at the beginning."

"We are all going on a picnic at City Park with Rose and her grandson. I invited you and Craig to join us. It's not a date if we are all going, right?" Mary Beth grinned.

"Yes, no, well, maybe," Angela said. She wasn't sure what the right answer was. She wanted to be supportive of her friend, but didn't know how. Was she supposed to be happy? Sad? Worried? Mad?

That week, Mary Beth found it hard to concentrate on work. She alternated between happiness at seeing Adam again, and fear of getting hurt again. Several times she picked up the phone and started to call and cancel the picnic. She still wasn't sure that she was doing the right thing, but she decided to follow through with her leap of faith.

God, I'm putting this in your hands. I don't know if this is a good idea, but I trust you and I want you to lead me.

After she prayed she felt better and refocused her attention on the task at hand. She was deep into a new project helping one of the other businesses in her building design and build a new filing system. It was nice that she didn't have to travel to see her client and lug her equipment around for a change. She was learning new tricks and techniques and inventing some of her own.

Saturday finally arrived. The girls met at their usual spot that morning. Mary Beth and Angela discussed how they expected the day to go. They planned out some emergency exit strategies, should they decide that things were going south. They also invented some secret signals so they could let each other know how they were doing without anyone else knowing. This made Mary Beth feel better and less panicked.

They had decided to take Mary Beth's Mini Cooper and have Craig meet them at the park. That way if things were going well, Angela and Craig could slip away. If Mary Beth suddenly needed to leave, Angela wouldn't be stranded either.

The day was beautiful. The Colorado sky was a deep blue. The temperature was in the mid-80s and there wasn't a cloud in the sky. The girls pulled into the parking lot and took out a blanket and cooler. They locked the car and looked around. Angela spotted her boyfriend and they waved him over. Craig greeted the girls and took the cooler. Soon they saw Adam pushing Rose in her wheelchair across the grass toward them.

After making introductions, the group made their way to the shade of a large oak tree next to the lake in the middle of the park. They spread the large blanket on the ground and set out the food. Adam helped Rose to the ground and leaned her against the trunk of the tree. They all made small talk as they went about the work. Soon they were ready to eat.

"Before we start, do you mind if we say grace?" Adam asked. Angela looked approvingly at Mary Beth. They all bowed their heads and Adam prayed. Mary Beth smiled to herself. *Chalk up one point for Adam.*

The meal went smoothly. Everyone talked easily about the park, the ducks, the weather. Stories were shared about their week. It was very relaxing. They watched other people in the park, playing with their kids, walking their dogs, riding their bikes.

Suddenly, Rose said, "That looks like fun!" Everyone followed her finger out over the water. They saw brightly colored paddle boats moving slowly across the lake.

"Grandma, I don't know if that's a good idea with your hip," Adam said.

"Oh, posh, we could at least go and look."

Everyone agreed that they would go to the dock and look at the boats. They quickly cleaned up the remains of the picnic and stowed them in their cars. Grandma Rose was reinstalled in her wheelchair and the group set off towards the boat ramp. When they arrived, they asked to rent a paddle boat. Angela and Craig took one boat and Adam helped Grandma Rose sit in another one. He sat beside her and tried out the foot pedals. They boat moved easily under his powerful legs. Mary Beth stood on the dock and took pictures of everyone with her phone. Seeing the smile on Grandma Rose's face made her feel good. She stood there, soaking in the sunshine, watching her friends on the water. *Thank you, Lord. I am glad I came. This is turning out to be a great day.*

Soon, Adam returned to the dock. He helped Grandma Rose out of the boat and into her chair. He found a patch of shade where she would be protected, but could still see the boats. He returned to the dock and Mary Beth. "Your turn," he said, gesturing to the boat.

"I don't know, I'm not really a water sport person," Mary Beth started. Then she stopped herself. Here was a hot guy, wanting to spend time with her, doing something romantic. "Scratch that. Let's do it!" She scrambled into the boat and sat down.

Adam grinned at her and climbed in beside her. They paddled out to the middle of the lake. It was calm and reflected the sky and trees around them. The ducks and geese weren't frightened off by the boats and swam around them.

Mary Beth stopped pedaling. Adam said, "What's wrong?"

"Nothing," Mary Beth responded. "I just wanted to look around and enjoy the view. I've never been out here before." She looked at Adam. He was smiling, too.

"Me neither. The view is amazing, isn't it?"

"Thank you, Adam," Mary Beth said.

"For what?"

"For today. For bringing us here. This was nice. I've had a great day with you."

"Your welcome," Adam said. He began pedaling again. They worked together in silence until they were back at the dock. Angela and Craig were already there and helped them out of the boat. Together they walked over to Rose. She smiled contentedly at them.

"Are you ready to go home, Grandma?" Adam asked her.

Rose nodded at him. She reached out and took Mary Beth's hand. "Thank you for coming today, Mary Beth. This was nice. I still want you to come over for that ice cream soon. Call me, ok?" She turned and said goodbye to Craig and Angela. Adam wheeled her off to his car while the others trekked across the grass to the parking lot on the other side of the park.

The girls hugged. Angela asked, "Did you have a good time?"

"I did! He's a pretty nice guy, don't you think?" Mary Beth replied.

"I really like him," Craig chimed in. "Much better than that loser, Cory. This guy has his life together. You can tell he loves his grandmother. That in itself should tell you what kind of person he is."

Angela nodded. "I agree. He is sweet. I like how he treats Rose. He is compassionate and kind. I can tell he thinks pretty highly of you, too, Mary Beth. The way he looks at you tells me he wants to get to know you better."

Mary Beth blushed and looked at her feet. "You're sweet. I think I'd like to get to know him better, too. I'm still a little scared, but knowing you two approve really helps."

Grandma Rose and Mary Beth had lunch and the promised ice cream the next Saturday. As if on cue, the doorbell rang just as they sat down to eat. Mary Beth opened the door on a familiar scene. Leaning against the door jamb was Adam, wearing his blue uniform. Her heart flip flopped, but for an entirely different reason this time. He smiled slowly at her and asked, "May I come in?"

Mary Beth nodded and stepped back. She didn't trust her voice, being so close to this handsome man. Adam walked past her and went to the kitchen. Mary Beth shut the door and followed him. The scent of his aftershave lingered in the air. She closed her eyes and breathed it in. *Focus, Mary Beth!* Opening in her eyes, she continued into the kitchen in time to see Rose hugging her grandson.

They sat at the table and joined hands. *I could get used to this.* Mary thought as Adam prayed. The conversation flowed easily from one topic to another. Adam started telling jokes that made them laugh out loud. The ice cream machine ground to a halt as if perfectly timed at the end of the meal. The dessert was smooth and silky and light. Grandma Rose had cut up some fresh strawberries to put on top. It was the perfect complement to the ice cream.

Much too soon lunch was over and Adam had to return to work. Mary Beth walked him out to his car.

"Mary Beth, can I ask you a question?" Adam asked.

"Sure," Mary answered.

Taking a deep breath, Adam said, "Would it be ok if I called you from my own phone sometime?"

Mary Beth laughed. "Yes, I'd like that."

"Would you give me your number, then?" Adam asked.

"Oh! Yes! That's right, you don't have it, do you?" Mary Beth put her hands to her face to hide her embarrassment. Quickly she recited the number while Adam put it into his phone.

After saying good-bye, she returned to the house. As she opened the door, she turned to wave. Adam was still standing by his patrol car, watching her. She waved to him and waited until he drove off before going inside. Butterflies were flitting around her stomach and she had a silly grin on her face.

"You look like the cat that swallowed the canary," Grandma Rose commented when Mary Beth entered the kitchen.

"I have a confession to make," Mary Beth told her. "I kinda like your grandson."

Rose laughed. "It's about time you realized that. You both have been trying to ignore your feelings ever since you met!"

"It's been that obvious?" She grabbed some dishes and took them to the sink. She didn't want Grandma Rose to see her pink cheeks.

"To me it is," she said gently, "because I know you both so well."

"Can I tell you something, Rose?" Mary Beth sat down across from the old woman. She started picking at her cuticles.

"Of course, you can," Rose answered.

"I'm scared," Mary Beth said. She told Grandma Rose the story of her last relationship and how hurt she had been. "I just don't want to put my heart on the line and get it crushed again."

Without saying a word, Grandma Rose took Mary Beth's hands in her own. Her arthritic thumbs gently stroked the backs of Mary Beth's hands. She sat for a moment looking down at the table. When she finally looked into Mary Beth's eyes, tears were streaming down her face. Mary Beth started to cry, too. Grandma Rose stood up and came around the table. She put her arms around the younger woman and held her. She stroked Mary Beth's hair and they cried together.

After a while, the tears abated, but still they clung to each other. Sobs turned to sniffles, and finally Mary Beth wiped her eyes with the backs of her hands. "Thank you, Rose. I needed that."

"You never deserved any of that, Mary Beth," Rose began. "No one should ever be treated that way. I can understand how you would feel very vulnerable right now. I can assure you, my grandson would NEVER treat a woman that way. And if he even THOUGHT about it, he would have to answer to me!" She made her way back to her seat and sat down. "I don't know about where you stand with God, but I know that He never wastes anything that happens to us. He uses our experiences to bring us closer to Him and to teach us to trust Him."

Mary Beth smiled a small smile. Her heart was beginning to heal, and this wonderful woman was a big part of that. *God never wastes anything that happens to us. I like that, I can see how He has been leading me this year through each of my leaps of faith.*

Mary Beth felt more confident about getting to know Adam with the knowledge that Grandma Rose had her back. She decided to fully commit to this leap of faith. She left the house with hope in her eyes and a spring in her step.

Vacation

  Mary Beth always looked forward to the month of August. For one thing, she loved school and couldn't wait to buy new school supplies. She loved the smell of paper and notebooks. Pens, pencils, rulers, protractors, you name it, shopping for these things made her happy. Now that she was finished with school, she really didn't have an excuse to go shopping for these things, but it was still fun to look. It didn't take much for her to find an excuse to buy SOME new things. She did have an office, after all, and office supplies were almost the same thing as school supplies.

  The other reason that she loved August so much was because it had become a tradition for Angela and her to take a vacation together at the end of summer break. Of course, now that they were business owners, there was no summer vacation, but it felt weird to not have a break. The two friends agreed that they should continue the tradition. For this year, they planned to spend it in Steamboat Springs. Neither of the girls had ever been there and it was only about a three-hour drive from Fort Collins. They planned to rent a condo for a week and take in the beauty of the Rocky Mountains, as well as a local wine festival. They combed the websites and planned out their trip with care. You would have thought they were taking an African safari, the amount of planning, packing, discussing and excitement they had.

The day before they were scheduled to leave, Angela went to a flea market and picked up some new pieces for her antique shop. She had found a bedroom set that included two night stands, a dresser, a bedstead, and a dressing table. Time was running out and she needed to get back to her apartment to finish packing, so she decided to unload her truck by herself. As she bent to pick up the last night stand, her back twisted in the wrong direction. Gasping in pain, she fell to her knees. Her back spasmed and she couldn't move. After about ten minutes, the pain subsided enough to where she managed to climb out of the back of the truck and find her phone.

Slowly, she maneuvered herself behind the wheel. She called Mary Beth as she drove to the doctor's office and explained what had happened.

Mary Beth met her at the chiropractor's office and helped her inside. The doctor examined her and adjusted her back. With a serious look on his face he put a hand on her shoulder. "Go home and alternate 20 minutes of ice with 20 minutes of heat tonight. I want to see you every day for the next five days."

Angela slowly made her way to the waiting room. Mary Beth stood up and went to meet her. Angela grimaced at Mary Beth. "I'm so sorry that I won't be able to make our trip," she said. "I can barely move and I have to come back to see Dr. Dave every day."

"We can cancel it and reschedule it for another time," Mary Beth offered.

"You are NOT canceling this vacation," Angela insisted, holding Mary Beth's shoulders. "You deserve to take a break from your work. I can't believe the crazy hours you have put in lately. I bet it's been over 80 a week these past two weeks. I can't travel like this, and you have booked yourself with clients practically 'til Christmas."

"I don't want to go by myself, though," Mary Beth argued back. "This was OUR vacation. I've never been on one by myself."

"Sounds like you are about to take another leap of faith, my friend," Angela said. "The condo is already booked, and the deposit is non-refundable. If you don't go, it will sit empty for the week and we'll be out that money. You might as well go and enjoy yourself."

"I don't know," Mary Beth replied. "What would I do all by myself?" She picked at her thumb as she spoke. "I don't know anyone up there."

Angela sighed. "You'll meet people, I promise. You just have to get out there and do stuff. Do everything we planned and take lots of pictures for me. I need to get home and lay down. You are going, and that is final." She turned slowly and made her way out of the office.

Mary Beth stood there, staring after her. Could she do this by herself? She'd never done anything, or gone anywhere, alone. *A leap of faith, alright. Didn't see that one coming.* She caught up with Angela and helped her into her truck. She followed Angela home and helped her get into bed with an ice pack. She made dinner and the two friends ate together.

Driving home, she said a prayer for Angela and her back. Then she said a prayer for herself. She finished her last-minute chores and packing. Soon the Mini Cooper was loaded and ready to leave. She gathered up all her itineraries and tickets and e-mail confirmations and put them in her computer bag.

The next morning, she was up early. It was another bright, beautiful Colorado day. It was only 6:30 and it already felt hot. The weather app on her phone promised that the temperature would soar to 100 by noon. Mary Beth looked around her tiny, yet organized, apartment. Nothing was out of place. She adjusted the blinds and shut all the windows. Taking a deep breath, she closed and locked the door, ready to start her adventure.

Heading up College Avenue, she encountered construction traffic. The city had been working on this project for at least three years. Luckily, it was early enough that Mary Beth didn't have to wait very long. Soon she was driving north, out of the city, towards the Poudre Canyon turn off. She loved taking her Mini Cooper up the canyon. The car was zippy and the road was twisty. The scenery was to die for, river, trees, canyon walls, aspen and pine trees. Many times Mary Beth and Angela had hiked, fished, and camped up here. Today was different, though. Mary Beth passed all the places where she had fond memories of times spent with family and friends.

Her little car zoomed up the canyon, over Cameron Pass at over 10,000 feet. The mountains looked spectacular with their peaks rising high against the blue sky. Dotted on their slopes were patches of white, still clinging to their hidden areas above timberline, where even the trees wouldn't grow. Soon she passed the tiny town of Gould. High grasslands spread around her. She reached the mountain town of Walden and turned past the cemetery.

Soon she arrived at Rabbit Ears Pass with its two summits. The first one the Mini Cooper climbed and descended with ease. *If I were in the postcard business, this would be the place to make money*, she thought, admiring the breathtaking beauty around her. The second summit was a little slower, with construction slowing traffic to one lane. *Typical Colorado,* Mary Beth mused, *can't go anywhere in the summer without some kind of construction delay.* The wait lasted almost ten minutes, and then the line of campers, trucks, and cars moved slowly across the pass. This side was VERY steep and Mary Beth kept having to use the brakes to keep her speed down. After a harrowing fifteen minutes, and a near death experience with an eighteen-wheeler, Mary Beth breathed a sigh of relief and entered Steamboat Springs.

Steamboat Springs was a beautiful mountain town surrounded by high mountains on all sides. The streets were lined with a quaint mixture of old and new architecture. The mountains were dotted with ski condos and expensive homes made of stone and logs. The ski area was hard to miss, with the runs cut in between swaths of trees. Even though it was summer, the gondolas were moving up and down the mountain.

Following her GPS, she quickly made her way up the side of one of the slopes to the street where her condo was located. The buildings were tan with brown trim. Each apartment had its own garage and all of the upper ones sported a balcony. In front of the one she and Angela had rented for the week was a small silver jeep. She parked on the street close to it and stepped out. A man climbed out of the jeep and came to meet her.

"Are you Angela, or Mary Beth?" the middle-aged man asked. He extended his hand. "Welcome to Steamboat Springs. I'm Tim. Let me show you around your condo." He took her up a flight of wooden steps to the second floor. He stopped in front of an open door and let her enter first.

The condo was decorated in neutral tones. The overstuffed couch and chairs faced a gas fireplace with a flat screen TV mounted above it. On either side were built in shelves. The shelves were tastefully filled with items related to skiing and mountain living. The small kitchen had a tall breakfast bar with stools. Down the hall were two bedrooms and two bathrooms. The tour lasted all of about three minutes. It was cute and cozy. Mary Beth wished, not for the first time that day, that Angela were with her. She listened to Tim give her directions on how to access the Wi-Fi, how to open the garage door, and where to take the trash when she was ready to leave.

When Tim finally left, Mary Beth sat heavily on the brown leather sofa. She was tired from the drive, and stressed at the prospect of spending five whole days alone in this place. *I could go to the grocery store and just hole up here for the week*, she told herself. She entertained the idea for a minute, then shook her head. *No, that would be wrong. I came here for a vacation, a leap of faith. If I stay inside the whole time, it would defeat the purpose!*

She forced herself up off the couch and out the door. She gathered her suitcase and computer case and hauled them up the stairs. She then spent some time arranging her clothes in the beautiful distressed wood dresser next to the king-sized bed and put all her toiletries in the bathroom. It felt a little more like home. Next, she set about investigating the kitchen. There were pots and pans and knives and dishes. The coffee maker even had a wake-up timer on it. *Thank you, God, for all of this. I'm impressed!*

She made a quick menu and a grocery list and set off to find the nearest grocery store. As she went back on the main thoroughfare into town, she found one. She pulled into the small parking lot, amazed at how, no matter where you went, you could always see the ski slopes. Today they were bright green streaks between darker green lines of trees. The gondolas reflected the sunlight as they swayed gently on their way up the mountain.

The store was laid out in a similar manner as the one back home, just on a smaller scale. She found what she needed in short order and was soon headed back to the condo. She unloaded the groceries and quickly made herself a simple lunch. As she munched on her sandwich and chips, she went over the itinerary that she and Angela had made the week prior.

I don't care what the itinerary says, Mary Beth thought, *the first thing I want to do is ride the gondola up to the top of the mountain.* She set her plate and knife in the sink and put away the lunch items. Gathering her camera and keys, she set off to find the base of the gondola operation. It wasn't very hard to find. In fact, it was close to where she had been grocery shopping. Before long, she was seated in the silver and blue enclosed capsule sailing upwards above the treetops towards the summit.

Mary Beth had grown up in Colorado and was used to the mountains, but the view from the gondola was breathtaking. She kept her face glued to the window the whole way up. On the top, she exited the gondola and took a deep breath. The fresh mountain air smelled of sun, wind, and pine trees. She smiled to herself and looked around. She found a hiking path and walked for an hour, pausing to take picture after picture. As the light began to fade, she made her way back to the gondola, feeling happy and relaxed.

On the way down the mountain, Mary Beth introduced herself to the people in the gondola car. "Hi," she said shyly. "Are you tourists, too?"

"Nah, we live here year-round," said the smiling young man. "I'm Hank, and this is my wife Yvonne."

They chatted the rest of the ride and Mary Beth learned about a few good places to hang out and even some advice on places to avoid. They invited her to come and hang out with them at a local favorite restaurant, but she was tired and decided to call it an early night. Pleased with her leap of faith progress, she went back to the condo, cooked dinner, cleaned up and went to bed.

The one bad thing about early bedtimes is that they usually lead to early wake ups. Mary Beth was awake with the sun the next day. She lay in bed for a long time, listening to the sounds of the world slowly waking up around her. The birds called to each other in the pink light, the aspen leaves whispered in the slight summer breeze and the pine trees swayed and creaked. It was a glorious morning.

Mary Beth took her breakfast out onto the balcony and received another surprise. There above the tree tops was a brightly colored hot air balloon hovering in the sky. It seemed to hang there, motionless. She caught her breath. Not long ago, at one of their Saturday breakfasts, she and Angela had compiled 'bucket lists', things they wanted to accomplish, do, and see before they died. Both of them had put 'ride in a hot air balloon' on their lists. Mary Beth went back inside and grabbed the copy of the Steamboat Springs visitor's guide that she had picked at the grocery store the day before. She flipped through it and found several ads for hot air balloon rides. Picking up her phone, she looked up the information on one of the companies and found that they operated daily from sunup until around eight o'clock each morning. She made the spur of the moment decision to schedule a ride.

A sense of satisfaction washed over her as she realized that she was being independent and making decisions for herself without being a fraidy cat or consulting anyone. It was a feeling she enjoyed and wanted more of.

Today's agenda included horseback riding and a bicycle ride. She packed up a lunch and water bottle filled with ice before she left the condo for the day. As she stepped off the stairs and onto the sidewalk she met several of her neighbors out walking their dogs. She met a pair of Great Pyrenees that were so tall they came above her knees. Their hair was super fluffy and white. They looked like walking marshmallows.

The day went by in a blur of horsehair and frantic pedaling. The fresh air and exercise was doing her a world of good. She realized that maybe she had been working a tad bit too hard. Mary Beth returned to the condo stiff, sore, and smelly. She was also smiling. After taking a long, badly needed shower, she decided to go into town and find the restaurant the locals had recommended the day before.

It took her a while to find the small eatery, as it was tucked into a side street, away from the showy touristy places. She walked in and to her surprise, Hank and Yvonne were there. They saw Mary Beth and waved her over to their table. She sat with them and had a great evening learning about Hank and Yvonne and their life in Steamboat Springs.

After dinner, Mary Beth made her way back to the condo, tired but happy.

I could get used to living here, she thought, looking over the valley, bathed in evening sunshine. She decided to walk around the neighborhood a little more before going to bed.

Each day, Mary Beth grew braver in her now familiar surroundings. She was able to greet several of the neighbors by name, and could find her way practically anywhere in the beautiful town without trouble.

Her hot air balloon ride was fantastic. She couldn't believe how quiet and peaceful it was. It made her feel very serene and calm. *This could be my happy place!* She enjoyed the vantage point of the balloon, looking down over the valley at the fields of hay and cattle as well as the historic buildings of the town. She kept busy with her camera as the world came into focus with the sunrise.

Her other adventures in the town and surrounding countryside were just as much fun. The week flew by in a flurry of activities and new faces. Mary Beth found herself looking forward to each new day with joyous abandon.

Even as she was enjoying herself, she never forgot about Angela. The two friends spoke on the phone every night and Mary Beth did her best to keep Angela abreast of her activities. She tried to be enthusiastic, yet not make Angela feel bad about not being there. Angela's back was healing slowly, and she promised that she was taking it easy, not lifting anything heavier than a soda can.

Before she knew it, the week was over and it was time to head back to reality. She packed up the Mini Cooper and added all of her souvenirs from her vacation. Each one brought a smile to her face. Lovingly packed in her suitcase were also several items she had purchased for Angela. Mary Beth had put a lot of thought into finding the perfect gift for her friend. Taking one last look around the cozy apartment, Mary Beth closed the door and headed out.

What is Love?

Mary Beth checked herself in the mirror one last time. She tugged at her shirt. She checked her teeth. She smoothed her hair. One more spritz of body spray, another smear of mascara. Finally, she stepped back and smiled. She touched the pendant hanging around her neck. She was ready.

Today she was going back to school. She couldn't believe it. Never in a million years did she imagine that she would be getting her master's degree! The butterflies in her stomach and the book bag by the door told her it was real.

School had always been fun for her, but that was when she knew everyone. She had felt confident in herself. This time it was definitely a leap of faith. She didn't know a single person at the college and 'master's degree' sounded hard. She wasn't sure that she could do this, but having an MBA would definitely give her a boost in running her own company.

She smiled as she picked up the book bag. Inside, in addition to the regular pencils, erasers, and notebooks, were some special items: a minion pencil bag from Adam, heart shaped sticky notes from Angela, and the bag itself from Grandma Rose. Yesterday, she had gone to Grandma Rose's house for lunch. When she had gone inside, she had been startled to see streamers, balloons and a big pink cake. Even more amazing was the fact that her entire family was there. Her mom, dad, and big sister had all come to wish her well.

She felt so loved and supported. It bolstered her resolve to go through with this degree. With any luck, she would be done in two years and her business would continue to thrive. She already felt somewhat successful, but didn't feel confident that she was doing the business side correctly. Her parents were big proponents of education, so she knew that she would have their approval in this adventure. They beamed at her all through lunch and asked tons of questions about her classes and what she would learn.

Her sister on the other hand, wasn't quite as enthusiastic. She gave Mary Beth her blessing, of course, but kept trying to interject into the conversation. She had always loved being the center of attention. Every time that Mary Beth was achieving something or excelling in school or work, Melody had to make sure that her parents knew what she was good at and what she had accomplished. It was very tiring, always having Melody playing 'one- up-man-ship'.

After a while, Mary Beth stepped outside into the back yard. She needed a break from her overbearing sibling, and a little space away from all the noise of the celebration. She was glad everyone was there, she just needed a minute to herself. She walked over to the patio chairs and lowered herself into one. She closed her eyes, feeling the warm sun on her face. She could hear the breeze playing with the leaves and the birds in the trees. She took several deep breaths and visibly relaxed into the cushions.

Hearing footsteps on the concrete, she opened her eyes. Standing in front of her, looking handsome in black jeans and a white shirt, was Adam. He was smiling down at her.

"What?" Mary Beth asked.

"Nothing," Adam replied, "just admiring the view. You looked very peaceful. Am I disturbing you?"

Mary Beth shook her head and patted the chair next to her. "Not at all. I just needed a break from all the noise in there. Come and join me."

Adam came over and sat next to Mary Beth. He leaned back and looked up at the deep blue sky. "I love it back here," he said. "There's something so peaceful about this place." He looked around the backyard. His gaze took in the old cottonwood trees, the green grass, the colorful flowerbeds, and the bird and squirrel feeders.

"I agree," Mary Beth said. "If I ever have a home of my own, I want to have a back yard like this. Grandma Rose spends so much time making it perfect." She turned her head toward the house, where she could hear laughter coming from the kitchen. She sighed. "I suppose I should go back in there. I don't know how much more of my sister I can take today. She is in rare form today, trying so hard to get my parents attention and trying to impress you and Rose."

"I noticed," Adam said. "She can't seem to stand back and let you have your moment. Is she always like that?"

Mary Beth nodded. "My whole life, she has been the center of attention. She is the favorite child and can't stand it if I do something better than her." She gestured towards the house. "This is perfectly normal. "

She started to stand up, but Adam put his hand on her arm and stopped her. She sat back and looked at him. "I want to give you one more gift," he said.

He handed her a square box wrapped in silver paper with a deep purple bow. Mary Beth took it with shaking hands. She looked at Adam. He was smiling at her. "Go ahead and open it!"

Slowly she slid the bow off the box. Then she turned the box over and carefully peeled the tape off. Opening the paper, she set it aside. Next, she opened the lid. Inside the box was a necklace. A silver butterfly outline was attached to a silver chain by one of the wings, making the butterfly appear to be flying. Inside one of the wing outlines were three small diamonds, arranged in a line.

Mary Beth gasped. "It's beautiful, Adam!"

"Just like you," Adam replied softly. "There is a lot of symbolism for me in this necklace. The butterfly is you. I know that we haven't known each other for very long, but I can see that you are an independent woman, just like a butterfly. It follows its own path and doesn't let anything get in its way. The three diamonds represent the past, the present, and the future. I hope you continue to pursue your passions."

"I don't know what to say. Thank you. This means a lot to me. YOU mean a lot to me. I'm so glad that we have gotten to know each other," Mary Beth said shyly. She reached over and squeezed his hand. He returned the squeeze and they stood up together.

"May I put the necklace on you?" Adam asked.

Mary Beth handed him the box, turned around and held up her curly brown hair. Adam slid the necklace around her neck. Mary Beth felt the cool metal on her skin. She fingered the butterfly. She had never received such a beautiful piece of jewelry from anyone, much less a man! She reached for Adam's hand and they walked back to join the noise inside.

Now the day had arrived. Mary Beth took her new school supplies and left her apartment. She walked toward her car and her heart sank. There, on the windshield was a piece of paper. *Oh, no! Not a parking ticket!* She walked closer and saw that it wasn't a ticket, but an envelope. Her name was hand printed on the outside. She slit open the envelope and found a card inside. On the front was a caterpillar holding a four-leaf clover saying 'Here's a lucky four-leaf clover for you'. Inside the caterpillar is pictured chewing on the clover saying, 'It was delicious!' The card was signed, 'You've got this! Love Angela'. Mary

Beth giggled. She tucked the card into her bag and headed off to the Colorado State University campus.

She arrived at the classroom ten minutes before class started. She pulled open the door and stepped in. She expected to find at least a dozen people taking up the seats facing the front of the room. She was surprised to find only five other people there. She double checked her schedule and the room number. She was in the right place. Puzzled, she found a seat and settled in. When the professor came in, Mary Beth's heart jumped to her throat. *Here we go! I hope I'm ready for this. God, prepare me for the challenges ahead.*

Class went smoothly. The professor gave everyone a syllabus and reading list. Everything in the packet looked doable. The only thing she was concerned about was the research project they were assigned. They had to pick what they wanted to research, rather than the teacher telling them what to do. It seemed backward, but the professor assured her that she would get more out of the project if she chose the topic.

At the end of the morning, Mary Beth called Angela to let her know how things had gone. She felt exhilarated and looked forward to all her classes. The jitters were gone and she was feeling very confident. For the rest of the day, Mary Beth was busy visiting some potential clients and returning phone calls.

That evening she attacked her assignments and read from her textbooks until bed time. As she was brushing her teeth, the phone rang. Looking at the screen, Adam's smiling face appeared. Quickly she rinsed her mouth and answered the call.

Adam and Mary Beth talked for quite a while. Mary Beth told Adam every detail of the day. Then she asked him about his day. He shared what he could about his day. Then he paused. "Mary Beth, I have something to tell you."

Mary Beth braced herself. The tone in Adam's voice told her that he had something serious to say. "What's wrong?" she asked.

"Nothing's wrong. I've just been thinking a lot about your 'leap of faith' experiment. I really like the idea and have decided to join you. I'm thinking about trying for a promotion in the department. I just wanted to get your opinion on it," Adam said.

Letting her breath out, Mary Beth said, "Oh, Adam! I think that's a great idea. I thought you had some bad news. This is the best of news. I'm so happy for you! What promotion is it?"

"I want to try for detective," Adam told her. "I've already filed my letter of intent. You have inspired me to step out of my comfort zone and stretch myself. I've been a patrol officer for five years. I'm pretty comfortable with what I'm doing. I don't want to become complacent."

Mary Beth encouraged Adam and promised to pray for his decision to follow God's lead. They said good night and Mary Beth climbed into bed, smiling happily.

The next few weeks flew by. The last Saturday of the month arrived and Mary Beth drove to Cooper as usual to have breakfast at Café on Main with Angela. The girls clung to their tradition as their lives became busier than ever. This time was an oasis for both of them, a time to check in and catch up. They took their time and savored every minute, as well as every bite. The small restaurant was a calm port in the storms of life. This Saturday was no different. Mary Beth claimed their usual spot and ordered for the both of them. She glanced at her phone and noticed that Angela was ten minutes late. It wasn't unusual, but Mary Beth felt that this was different.

When twenty minutes had gone by and no Angela, Mary Beth picked up her phone and texted her friend. No reply. A bad feeling settled in Mary Beth's stomach. She signaled for Sandy, the waitress. "Could I please get a to go box?"

Quickly, she gathered up breakfast and headed out. First, she checked Angela's antique store. The lights were out and the doors were locked. Mary Beth sprinted to her car, calling Angela as she ran.

The phone rang and rang, and finally went to voicemail. Now, real panic started to set in. It wasn't like Angela to not answer her phone or texts. *Maybe her battery died. Maybe she put it on silent.* Her gut told her that wasn't the case.

She tried to keep the Mini Cooper at the speed limit, but every time she looked down, it had inched higher. Mary Beth leaned forward as she drove. She was praying and panicking at the same time. The fifteen minutes it took to get to Angela's house seemed to last for an eternity. She checked the garage and saw Angela's car. It made her feel a little better, but at the same time, brought new questions and fears to mind.

Mary Beth ran up the stairs to the porch and pounded her fist on the door. She paused to catch her breath and leaned her ear against the door. "Angela?" she called out. She didn't hear anything. She tried the door handle, but it didn't move. Reaching into her purse she pulled out a keyring with a pink unicorn on it. Using her spare key, she let herself into the apartment, calling out Angela's name. The curtains were all pulled closed. There was a gloom about the place. Flipping on the lights, she looked around. There were wads of white tissues all over the floor. Mary Beth followed the trail of used Kleenex.

She found Angela huddled on the floor next to her bed. She was sobbing and limp. Mary Beth dropped to her knees next to her and gathered her in her arms. She held Angela and stroked her hair until she calmed down. Still not letting go, she asked, "What happened?"

Angela shuddered. She reached her arms around Mary Beth and buried her face in her friend's shoulder. Slowly, the story came out.

Angela had received a phone call from her mother that morning. Her mom had been frantic and it took a few minutes before it became clear what was going on. Angela's grandma had passed away. She sank to the floor in her living room. Tears streamed down her face. As she listened to her mom, sobs wracked her body. She felt numb. Her grandmother had been a big part of her life. Her mom had worked a lot when she was little, being a single mom. Angela had spent every day after school at her grandmother's house. Summers were spent splashing in the kiddy pool in her back yard and helping her in her large garden. Having her gone was losing a life line. Angela relied on her grandmother for relationship advice and encouragement in all of her life decisions. The bottom dropped out of her world, knowing she had died. Somehow, she had managed to make it to her bedroom before she had completely broken down.

Mary Beth helped Angela onto a chair and went to find a glass of water. She found Angela's phone halfway under the couch. No wonder she hadn't returned her texts and calls.

Angela allowed Mary Beth to wipe her face with a cool damp washcloth. She sipped at the water. Color slowly returned to her ashen face and her sobs slowed. Through puffy eyes, she looked at her best friend. "What am I going to do?" she asked, fresh tears staining her cheeks.

Mary Beth's eyes welled up. "I don't know. Right now, you are going to get in the shower and then you are going to eat something." She helped Angela to the bathroom and started the shower for her. She closed the door and listened. As soon as she was sure Angela had gone under the water, she picked up her phone and dialed Angela's mother.

"Hi, Mrs. Radcliffe, it's me, Mary Beth. I just found out about Grandma Jean and I'm here with Angela. I am SO sorry for your loss."

She kept the conversation brief, knowing that everyone would be wanting to call and speak with the family. She asked for the pertinent information about the funeral. Before she hung up, she promised to keep Angela company and help her through her grieving.

Hearing the water turn off, Mary Beth walked to the kitchen and got out plates and cups. She started the coffee machine and reheated the cinnamon roll in the microwave. Soon Angela wandered into the kitchen wearing a t-shirt and sweatpants. Her hair was dripping and her eyes were swollen, but her step was a little lighter.

The girls sat at the table and Mary Beth took Angela's hands in her own. They bowed their heads and prayed over the food, over the family, and over their lives. "Amen," they said together and hugged tight. A few bites of pastry were all Angela could manage, but she did drink the coffee. The girls spoke about their memories of Grandma Jean. Mary Beth had traveled to Grand Junction several times with Angela to spend time with her. They both remembered picking apples in her back yard and making applesauce. They had gone to the dinosaur museum in Fruita multiple times through the years. Their favorite times were lying on their backs at night in the cool grass, looking at the stars. Grandma Jean could tell the best stories.

"Let's get you packed," Mary Beth said. "We need to get on the road before too long. You know how bad traffic can be on the weekends on I-70."

"We? You are coming with me?" Angela asked.

"Of course, I am," Mary Beth insisted. "I don't want you to have to do this alone. You are in no condition to drive that far by yourself."

Angela shook her head. "But what about your classes and your schoolwork? You can't miss that! And your clients. You are booked solid until Christmas!"

"I'll e-mail my professors and take my laptop with me. No big deal. This is more important. I'll call my clients and reschedule. I'm sure they'll understand. And if they don't, well, I don't need people like that in my life anyway," Mary Beth insisted, directing Angela towards her bedroom.

Half an hour later, the girls had packed Angela's suitcase and loaded it into the Mini Cooper. They drove over to Mary Beth's house and did the same there. Soon they were zooming down the interstate towards Denver. Mary Beth glanced sideways at her best friend. Angela was staring straight ahead through the windshield, not seeing anything. It broke her heart to see her hurting so badly. *Lord, watch over us today. Keep us safe on this trip, and comfort Angela and her family in this time of need. Give me the right words to say to be of help to them.*

The miles passed quickly and soon the speedy little car was zooming up Vail Pass. Mary Beth decided that she had better call Adam to let him know what was happening. Her car had blue-tooth and so she put him on speaker. After filling him in on all the details, Mary Beth told him they would be home sometime on Wednesday. She promised to call him back after they had arrived in Grand Junction.

The rest of the five-hour journey passed uneventfully and the girls arrived at Angela's parents' house in the middle of the afternoon. The quiet street was packed with cars. There were friends and relatives milling around the yard, and coming and going from the house. Mary Beth found a spot to park about a block from the house. As they walked toward the front door they were stopped multiple times by various relatives wanting to hug Angela.

Inside the house was crazier than outside. Every chair in the living room was filled and people were standing around. Conversations were quiet and sounds of sobbing could be heard everywhere. Making their way through the throng, Angela kept asking for her mother. They were directed to the kitchen and upon arriving there, they found her, leaning over the oven, pulling out a pie.

"Mom!" Angela cried and ran to her. Mrs. Radcliffe quickly set the hot pie on a cooling rack and turned. The two grabbed each other and began crying. Everyone in the room stopped talking and gathered around them. The huddle of women remained still for a long time, quietly sobbing and holding each other. Mary Beth could sense the love in the room. It was so tangible that you could almost see it. *This is what family is supposed to be like*, she thought to herself, soaking it in.

After a while, the crying slowed and the women pulled themselves apart. No one went very far, though. They all stayed nearby, lending their strength to Angela and her mother. Two chairs were vacated at the kitchen table and mother and daughter sat down together. Willing hands took over the tasks of cooking and cleaning.

The rest of the afternoon passed in a blur of tears, hugs, and condolences. Mary Beth did her best to be there for her friend and not be in the way. Everyone around her treated her like she was a part of the family. By evening, most of the crowd had cleared out and the family was alone at last. They sat down at the table and ate some of the dishes that neighbors and friends had delivered. The refrigerator and countertops were groaning under the loads of food that had shown up during the day.

Mrs. Radcliffe kept reaching for the girls' hands and squeezing them. "I am so glad you came so quickly," she said several times. "I don't know how I'm going to make it through the next few days. Oh, Angela, I missed you and needed you."

"I'm here now, Mama," Angela said, hugging her mother. "We'll do it together."

That night Mary Beth didn't get much sleep. She was awakened repeatedly by Angela's tossing and turning, and Mrs. Radcliffe's pacing up and down the hall. It was a relief when they both settled down and slept toward the early morning.

Sunday was another hard day for all the family. The aunts and uncles and cousins all came over again to help plan the funeral. Scrap books and photo albums were pulled out and pictures chosen to be scanned into a slide show of Grandma Jean's life. Music was selected to go with the pictures. One of the uncles had brought his computer and was put in charge. Minor squabbles over the service were handled by the pastor, who also came and spent the afternoon with the family. The tears were lessened by the stories that everyone told about

Grandma Jean. A few smiles appeared, and even a chuckle or two over some of the antics that Grandma liked to pull.

Mary Beth kept busy filling coffee cups and emptying the dishwasher. Finger foods were set out and picked at throughout the day. By evening, everyone was feeling drained from the intense emotions they were feeling. No one felt much like eating dinner and everyone went to bed early. Mary Beth went outside to make her nightly call to Adam.

When he picked up the phone, Mary Beth could hear a strange whistling sound in the background. "Where are you?" she asked tiredly. "It sounds weird."

The sound lessened and Adam asked, "Is that better?"

"Yes. I can hear you better. What was that?"

"I had the window down in my car. Sorry about that. How was your day?" Adam replied.

Mary Beth told him about the funeral arrangements for Monday and how the family was coping with everything. "They all went to bed early, so I thought this would be a good chance to talk to you uninterrupted."

"That's good, they need their rest. Tomorrow is going to be rough." There were voices in the background, but Mary Beth couldn't hear what they were saying.

"Who are you with?" she asked.

"Oh, just a couple of people you know; Grandma Rose and Craig, Angela's boyfriend," he replied.

"What are you doing with them?" Mary Beth asked.

"We're coming to Grand Junction for the funeral," Adam said. "We didn't want you to be alone in all this. We're just about to Palisade right now, so we'll be there in the next half hour or so. I've already booked rooms for us at the Holiday Inn."

Mary Beth stood, slack jawed. *How in the world did I land a boyfriend like this?* She thought to herself. *This is amazing. God, YOU are amazing. I don't deserve this, but thank you!*

"Wow. I can't believe this," she said aloud. "I never expected you to come all the way to the Western Slope to be with me. Thank you. This will mean so much to Angela, too, I'm sure."

"Hey, that's what we're here for. We support the ones we love, right?" Adam said, gruffly. "I'll call you when we get settled in at the hotel, ok?"

Support the ones we love? That was a loaded sentence. Mary gulped, "Ok," and hung up the phone. She sat down on a rocking chair on the porch and watched the light fade from the sky. Did she hear Adam right? Did he mean that he loved her? Or was he talking about Craig loving Angela? Her head hurt from the emotion filled day. She shook her head. *I don't have the energy to analyze this right now.*

Soon, her phone rang. The trio had made it to town and were safely ensconced in their hotel. Adam asked Mary Beth if she had eaten dinner. She thought about it for a second and then realized that, no, she hadn't had more than a few bites all day. Taking care of the family had been a full-time job and she hadn't stopped to take care of herself.

She agreed to join Craig, Adam, and Grandma Rose at a local steak house. She ran inside and grabbed her keys. She paused in the kitchen to write a note, just in case anyone needed her. Then she headed out the door.

The steak place was one of those rustic, Texas-style places with boots, hats, and ropes arranged as decorations on the walls. The tables were wagon wheels with a piece of plexi-glass over the top. Country music blared from a jukebox and the wait staff all wore bandanas around their necks. Adam waved Mary Beth over to their table in the back. He had already ordered her an iced tea. She sat down heavily, smelling the aroma of freshly baked bread. Her stomach growled suddenly. She reached for a roll and smeared butter on it. The bread was still warm and it was just the right amount of crusty on the outside and doughy on the inside. She closed her eyes and sighed.

"Rough day?" Adam asked.

Mary Beth nodded and told everyone what was happening at the Radcliffe home. She talked about the funeral service and the slide show and the family dinner afterwards. "Angela is doing much better today than she did yesterday. She is still a mess, but she is able to at least function and hold a conversation now. She is trying to be strong for her mother. Both of them really depended on Grandma Jean. I don't know what they will do now that she's gone." Mary Beth blew out a big breath and tried to contain her emotions.

Craig said, "We are here for them, and you, too, Mary Beth." Grandma Rose nodded.

"You don't know how much I appreciate you all coming," Mary Beth managed. "This has been so hard. I don't know what to do, or say, or anything. Mostly I'm just trying not to be in the way."

Grandma Rose took Mary Beth's hand between her rough, arthritic ones. "You are doing everything exactly right. You are being supportive of Angela in the best way you know how. She probably doesn't have the emotional capacity to recognize it right now, but I know that she appreciates everything you are doing for her." She squeezed Mary Beth's hand.

The group of friends ate and talked for a long time. Grandma Rose finally said, "Mary Beth, you look exhausted. We should let you get some rest. We all should. We need to be at our best tomorrow for Angela and her family."

Mary Beth nodded sleepily. The food had finally caught up with her and she was fading fast. Craig, Adam and Grandma Rose each gave Mary Beth a hug and promised to come over to the house in the morning and bring the family breakfast.

Mary Beth drove back to the house and let herself in. She tiptoed past Mrs. Radcliffe's room and heard the sound of steady breathing. She continued on to Angela's room and was relieved to hear the same even sound. She readied herself for bed and slipped between the cool sheets. *Thank you, Lord, for such a great gift tonight.* Her eyes closed and she drifted off to sleep.

The next morning, everyone was in a very somber mood. The women met in the kitchen and sat around the table. Mary Beth poured cups of coffee for everyone. There wasn't much conversation. They stared into their cups and each was lost in her thoughts.

The doorbell rang and Mary Beth told Angela that she should go and answer it. A small smile played around her lips as she listened to Angela's footsteps approach the door. She stood up and slowly followed her into the living room. She wanted to see Angela's reaction when she saw who was at the door.

"Craig!" Angela exclaimed. She grabbed him and pulled him into a bear hug. "I missed you so much! You're here! I can't believe it! I didn't think you were going to be able to come!" She continued to gush, then realized Craig wasn't alone. She let go of Craig and squeezed Adam in another bear hug. She saw Grandma Rose behind him and grabbed her and pulled her into her arms. Tears flowed down her cheeks, this time for a different reason. She was so touched that these people had come to her in her time of need. She felt so loved and wanted it swelled her heart.

Angela ushered the group into the kitchen and made the introductions to her mother. Everyone hugged Mrs. Radcliffe and offered their condolences. They presented the boxes of pastries they had brought for breakfast. Plates and forks appeared, and everyone gathered around the table. Grandma Rose offered the blessing and prayed a special prayer for the family on this difficult day. Mrs. Radcliffe thanked her and gave her a hug.

Over breakfast, everyone made small talk to fill the time. Everyone was watching the clock, dreading the time that they would have to make their way to the church. Unfortunately, that time came sooner than anyone was ready for.

The group crowded into two cars and headed for the funeral. They filed into the church and signed the guest book. As they made their way to the front pews in the sanctuary, Angela grabbed her mother's arm on one side and Mary Beth's on the other. They walked together down the aisle. There at the front was Grandma Jean's casket, draped in white roses and day lilies. The room was filling up quickly and Angela and her mother huddled together with the rest of their family.

During the service, the pastor gave a beautiful message about death being a beginning, not an ending, for those who know the Lord. He ended his message by offering to pray the prayer of salvation for those who wanted to become Christians. After he spoke, Angela's mother got up and gave the eulogy. There wasn't a dry eye in the place. Everyone was there to celebrate the life of a wonderful woman. The slide show ran in a loop, showing pictures from every phase of Grandma Jean's life. The family stood to receive the mourners as they filed past the casket to say good bye to her.

Mary Beth sat in her seat and watched her friend. She looked small and vulnerable, but at the same time strong and resilient. Mary Beth held Adam's hand and cried unashamedly. After everyone had gone out of the sanctuary, several of Mrs. Radcliffe's male relatives closed the casket and took it to the hearse. The family had decided to have a private burial after the memorial service. They followed the hearse to the cemetery and said their good-byes there.

The family congregated back at Mrs. Radcliffe's house that afternoon. They laid out all the food that had been so generously donated by members of the church for this meal. People spilled out onto the backyard lawn to enjoy the late September sunshine. Mary Beth and Adam found a quiet corner and sat on the grass. They each had a paper plate filled with macaroni salad, roast beef, rolls and other buffet items. They munched in silence as they watched the other people around them.

"Adam," Mary Beth started, hesitantly, "thank you for coming to this. It means a lot to Angela that you brought Craig and Grandma Rose."

"Your welcome," Adam replied. "I can't imagine how painful it must be to lose someone close to you. It was hard enough when Grandma Rose fell and broke her hip."

Mary Beth nodded her head. "I'm not that close to my grandparents, they live far away, but your grandmother has become like family to me. I was so afraid that she was going to die when she fell."

"So was I," Adam admitted. He picked at some blades of grass for a minute. "Mary Beth, you have made such a huge difference in my grandma's life. She struggled for years to get on with her life after my grandfather passed away. You brought her back to us. Thank you for that."

Mary Beth blushed. She didn't know what to say. "I...thank you…. It was… I mean… working with Rose was a challenge, to begin with. Then I turned it into a leap of faith. I prayed that God would show me how to reach her and help her. And He did."

"I really love your leap of faith idea," Adam said. "It seems to be changing you, for the better, I mean. You are a more confident woman, more of a risk taker, even in the short time we've known each other. It's very inspiring! And not just to me. Grandma Rose was talking about it yesterday on the drive over here."

"She was? I am?" Mary Beth said.

"Yes," Adam laughed, "she was and you are. She is thinking of taking a small leap of her own. It seems that the senior community in Fort Collins is quite active. She is going to join them for their game night next week. A year ago, we couldn't even get her out of the house to go to dinner."

"Wow, I didn't realize that I was rubbing off on people. That's great. I am so proud of Grandma Rose. She is such an amazing person," Mary Beth said.

"My ears are burning. Are you two talking about me?" Grandma Rose asked walking up beside them.

Adam stood up and Mary Beth joined him. He went off in search of a chair. Mary Beth said, "Adam was telling me that you are going to take a leap of faith next week. "

Grandma Rose hugged Mary Beth. "Yes, I am. I've been inspired by this project of yours. I am going to get out of the house and meet some new people, try some new things."

Mary Beth said, "I didn't know what to do to help you when we started, so I spent a lot of time praying that I would find the right way. Turns out, God had a plan in the works. I just listened."

"I'm so glad you did, dear," Grandma Rose said, sitting in the chair Adam set down for her in the shade. They sat in the grass in front of her.

The afternoon passed slowly. Angela's family stayed until nearly dark. Mary Beth, Grandma Rose, Adam and Craig all pitched in to clean up after everyone was gone. After taking out the last bag of garbage, Adam asked about Mary Beth and Angela's plans for returning to the Front Range.

Mary Beth looked at Angela questioningly. She wanted her friend to take the time she needed to be with her family, and not push her to return to Fort Collins too quickly. Angela turned to her mother.

"Mom, what do you need help with? I don't want to leave you stranded here."

Mrs. Radcliffe looked around at the circle of faces. She let out a tired sigh. "I can't think of anything right now. I'm too exhausted to think straight."

Everyone agreed that they felt the same way. They decided to call it a night and to continue the discussion in the morning over breakfast at The Chicken and the Egg restaurant.

The cheerful yellow walls and homey atmosphere at the restaurant made everyone feel a little better. When the food arrived, they all found that their appetites had returned. The table was quiet for a few minutes while the group took their first bites of food. Soon, though, the conversation began to flow. More stories about Grandma Jean were the general theme of the day.

"Mom, do you remember the time that Grandma took us out to see the headless chicken farm?" Angela asked. "I was so grossed out I almost became a vegetarian!"

Craig choked on his orange juice. "Headless chicken farm? What is this, Sleepy Hollow?"

Mrs. Radcliffe chuckled. "No, nothing like that. There was a farmer way back in the day that went to butcher a chicken for dinner. He cut off the chicken's head, but instead of just flopping around for a little while, this particular hen got up and walked around. They decided to keep the chicken around and actually made quite a bit of money off it as a side show attraction. There's even an annual festival honoring it."

"No kidding? That's the strangest thing I've ever heard of," Craig said, shaking his head.

"Grandma Jean loved to find out of the way places like that. She was quite the explorer. We went on many adventures like that," Angela added. "She liked to collect odd pieces she would find, too. She has several one of a kind things in her home."

Turning to her mother, she asked, "Speaking of Grandma's house, what is going to happen to it?"

"I don't know," Mrs. Radcliffe said softly. "I need some time to think about it. I suppose it falls to me to decided, doesn't it?"

Grandma Rose laid her hand on Mrs. Radcliffe's arm. "Take all the time you need. Don't let anyone rush you into making any decisions right now."

"Do you want me to stay and help you with anything, Mom? I'm here for you," Angela said.

"You have all been such a wonderful blessing. Thank you for helping with everything. I think I'll be alright. You should go home. I know you all have lives to get back to. I spoke with my brothers yesterday after the funeral and they are going to stick around and help me with Grandma Jean's house. We are going to take it slow."

They all finished their breakfast and Adam paid the bill. He insisted that it was the least he could do. Craig, Adam and Grandma Jean headed back to the hotel to check out. Mary Beth and Angela headed back to her mother's house to pack up.

It had been decided that Craig and Angela would drive back in Adam's car, while Mary Beth, Adam and Grandma Rose would take the Mini Cooper. That way Craig and Angela could have some time alone to process the events of the past few days.

The trip went smoothly. Being a week day, the traffic wasn't nearly as heavy on the interstate. The caravan made good time and arrived back in Fort Collins just before dinner time. First, they dropped off Grandma Rose, promising to come and see her in the next couple of days. Then they drove to Angela's apartment. She and Craig were going to spend a quiet evening there before Angela drove him home.

That left Adam and Mary Beth with their two cars. They agreed to drive to her apartment and order a pizza. They were both tired from driving but wanted to spend some time together.

They opened all the windows to let the fresh air blow away the stale, closed up smells of the apartment while they waited for their meal to arrive. Mary Beth hauled her suitcase into her bedroom and dumped it in a corner. "I'll take care of it tomorrow," she said.

When dinner arrived, they sat on the couch and watched a rerun of Gilligan's Island. It felt nice to be together, not needing to say anything for a while.

Soon the pizza and soda were gone. Mary Beth turned off the TV. She readjusted herself on the couch so she could look Adam in the eyes. "Thank you again for coming to the funeral. That was really sweet of you."

"You're welcome, Mary Beth," Adam said.

Mary Beth picked at her cuticles, the way she always did when she was nervous or stressed out. Taking a deep breath, she said, "That comment you made the other day, about doing things for people you love, um, what did you mean?" Mary Beth looked at the floor as she talked.

"I mean exactly what you think I mean. I love you Mary Beth." Adam put his hand under her chin and lifted her face. The look in his eyes was one of tenderness and concern. "I would drive to the ends of the earth to be with you. What is important to you is important to me. You mean more to me than anything."

Mary Beth looked into his eyes and her heart melted. She couldn't believe that only a few months ago she had been a blubbering mess over a man who didn't care about her at all. Now here she was, with a handsome police officer, who said he loved her.

"I love you, too, Adam," she said quietly. "I have never met a man like you. "

Adam took her hand and sparks shot up her arm, through her heart and made fireworks in her brain. She blushed a deep red and looked down at her feet. *I can't believe this is happening!* She thought. She felt Adam scoot closer to her and she looked up, tucking her hair behind her ear. She leaned in and met Adam's lips with her own. It felt so right, being here with him. Her heart started to pound.

They pulled away and Adam touched her face with his fingers. "I love the way you blush," he said. "Pink is a very becoming color for you."

Mary Beth giggled and pushed his hand away. She turned away from him and stood up. "That's not fair! I can't be anywhere near you without getting all flustered and hot."

"I'll have to remember that," Adam teased, standing up and coming towards her. He put his arms around her waist and kissed her again. "Let's see if we can keep you 'in the pink'."

Stage Fright

Life settled into a routine for Mary Beth. She was up early every morning working on writing papers and reading text books. She was out the door by 7:30 to get to CSU and had classes generally until noon. Running home for a quick bite to eat, she was at the office by 12:45, listening to her voicemail, checking her e-mails, returning calls, setting up appointments.

Her afternoons were filled with meeting clients and working on their various projects. Some of them only took her a few hours, while others were much more extensive, taking days, and sometimes even weeks.

Evenings were usually reserved for time with Adam. They had been officially dating for only a few weeks, but she missed him when he had to work late. They tried to see each other every day, if they could, but both of them were busy with studying. Adam's bid for a promotion had been approved and now he had to sit for a test and an interview with the lieutenant in charge of detectives. He was nervous and Mary Beth helped him study when he came to her apartment for dinner. He, in turn, helped her study for her exams and proofread her papers.

Saturday mornings were still spent with Angela, eating giant cinnamon rolls and keeping each other up to speed with life.

"What's up, lady?" Mary Beth said, sliding onto a chair in the back corner of the restaurant.

"Not much, girlfriend," Angela returned, leaning over to hug her friend. "It's been a great week in the antique business, or should I say 'mantique' business." She added air quotes for emphasis.

"What's that?" Mary Beth questioned.

"I've found quite a market for antiques for men. You know, oil cans, hood ornaments, gas pumps. Man-tiques, they're called." Angela had expanded her business to the internet. She still kept her inventory at the store, but now she was marketing over the computer. "I can't keep my inventory up! I can't find things fast enough to keep the shelves full."

Mary Beth laughed. "What a great problem to have. I'll have to ask my dad if he has any 'inventory' lying around the garage. My mom would probably say yes, but I'll ask Dad first."

"Would you? Ask Adam, too. I know he's a car nut. I need to find some new sources or start knocking on these farmer's doors." Angela was getting animated at the thought of fresh antiques.

"How has your week been, busy pants?" Angela asked.

Mary Beth's expression changed immediately. "Not so good," she said glumly.

Angela leaned forward, concern on her face. "What's wrong? Did your sister do something? Are you and Adam OK?"

"It's nothing like that," Mary Beth assured her. "It's school. One of my assignments. I have to get up in front of my class and make a speech. I don't think I can do it. Every time I think about it, I feel like throwing up. You know how much I hate being in the spotlight." She looked at Angela with pleading eyes. "If I don't do it, I fail the class. If I do it, I'll fail for sure! I'm sunk!"

Angela took Mary Beth's hands in her own. She looked at the fingers. Sure enough, there were spots where Mary Beth had picked at her cuticles so badly that the skin was torn and raw. She sighed and said, "I know that this has you stressed out completely. First, we are going to get you some band aids, and then we are going to conquer this fear."

Mary Beth shook her head vigorously. "I can't. Don't you remember what happened in high school? Mrs. Borah's English class? I passed out and had to be carried to the nurse's office. I can't do this!" Her face was red and she was beginning to hyperventilate.

"Whoa, whoa," Angela said. "Slow down! When do you have to give the speech? Not tomorrow, I hope."

"Three weeks," Mary Beth groaned. "I think I'll just drop the class."

"No, you're not," Angela said, firmly. "You have to face this. Besides, it's too late. Isn't it past the drop date."

"In that case, I'm going to fail the class!" Mary Beth said, her face still red and blotchy. The more she thought about the prospect of people staring at her, the sicker she felt. She took a sip of iced tea and tried to calm down.

Angela also took a drink and a bite of cinnamon deliciousness. She watched as Mary Beth tried to get her emotions under control. She had never seen her friend have such a strong reaction to anything. Usually she was a can-do person. This was definitely a different side of Mary Beth, and not a pretty one.

"How about starting by writing the speech as if it were just another paper?" she suggested. "That part's not hard, is it?"

"No," agreed Mary Beth. "I can write papers in my sleep. I've done so many this semester, they're practically coming out my ears!"

"Good, then that's what you'll do. Just pretend that it's another one of those assignments. How long will that take you?" Angela encouraged.

Mary Beth looked up at the ceiling. "About two days," she said. "That's not the same as writing a speech, though."

Angela nodded. "I know," she said. "But I have a plan. You just write the speech, I mean paper, and bring it to my house on Monday night."

The girls finished their breakfast and parted ways. Mary Beth agreed to go home and get started on the assignment. She was very skeptical, but also very curious about this plan Angela had. Knowing that her friend was going to help her calmed her down a little bit, but she shuddered every time she remembered the embarrassment she had felt in that high school English class.

As agreed, Mary Beth showed up at Angela's house, paper in hand, on Monday evening. She rang the doorbell and waited. Soon Angela let her in. "I've made chef salads for dinner," she told her, leading the way to the kitchen. She took Mary Beth's paper from her and deposited it in the office and shut the door. "Let's eat before we get to that. No one is going to do their best work while they are hungry," she said.

Mary Beth agreed and the two friends sat and chatted over their dinner. It wasn't as relaxing as it usually was. Mary Beth felt like the speech was standing behind her, waiting to grab her by the throat with its icy hands. Nervously, she shifted in her seat and glanced at the closed office door.

Angela saw Mary Beth's discomfort and suggested that they start on phase two of the project.

"Mary Beth, think of this as a leap of faith," she suggested. "You have done so well this year, overcoming obstacles, stretching yourself. This is a great opportunity for you to overcome this fear you have."

"I know," Mary Beth sighed. "It's just...well...I don't...um... this one's hard for me. I have a lot of emotional baggage around this issue. I never could live down that speech and it has haunted me ever since."

The girls cleared their dishes and headed into the office. They sat down together at the desk. Angela opened the top drawer and pulled out a stack of note cards. She explained her idea to Mary Beth. "We'll take your paper and split it into smaller chunks, using highlighters, and then rewrite the chunks on these cards."

"That sounds easy enough," Mary Beth said, reaching for a pink highlighter.

They spent the better part of an hour going over the paper and writing out the note cards. When they finished, they had a stack of cards about an inch thick. Angela gathered the stack and tapped it on the desk to align the cards.

"Whoa, that's a lot of cards!" Mary Beth exclaimed. "That looks like it would be an hour-long speech! I'm not talking for THAT long!" She covered her face with her arms and laid her head on the desk.

Angela patted her on the back. "We aren't finished yet. Phase Three happens tomorrow night. You have done plenty for one night! I'm proud of you! See? Small steps. That's all it takes."

Mary Beth gathered her purse and said good night. She was tired. It was exhausting trying to conquer your fears. She promised to be back the following night.

Art supplies covered Angela's dining room table when Mary Beth arrived the next evening. There were several pieces of poster board, paintbrushes, even glitter. She looked at Angela questioningly. "What's all this? Arts and crafts?"

"You'll just have to wait and see," Angela replied mysteriously. She smiled and ushered Mary Beth into the back yard, where she had set the picnic table with a colorful cloth and dishes. The girls dined alfresco, enjoying the cool evening air. They ate hot dogs and beans, chips and macaroni salad.

"Okay, now will you tell me what we're doing?" Mary Beth asked as they brought all the dishes into the kitchen.

"Follow me," Angela said and walked to the large, antique dining room table. She had placed a plastic table cloth over the wood. She handed Mary Beth an old shirt to cover her clothes. "We are going to make posters of your three most important points," she said triumphantly. "We can make them with any of the materials you see here. I also have a stash of stickers and even a few balloons, should you choose to use them. You said that there were too many cards, so this way you <u>have</u> to narrow down your focus and choose the three things you really want your audience to know."

She pulled out the large stack of note cards from the night before and handed them to Mary Beth. Mary Beth slowly reached for them, with much less enthusiasm than her friend.

"Oooookaaaaay," she said slowly. "How am I going to do that?"

"Either you read through the cards and pick what you want, or I'm throwing the cards in the air and you pick up the first three you see hit the floor. Your choice," Angela said with a devilish smile.

"Fine, I'll pick, although I'm tempted to try your second way," Mary Beth said, returning the smile. Soon she had narrowed down her points to the top three. The next hour and a half flew by as the girls became engrossed in the project.

"This is actually fun," Mary Beth admitted. "You, my dear, are one creative chica!" At the end of the evening, there were three colorful posters illustrating Mary Beth's main points propped on dining room chairs to dry. They stood back and admired their handiwork.

"That was phase three of the mission," Angela said, in her best James Bond voice. "Return tomorrow for phase four, if you dare!"

Mary Beth giggled at the impression. "Now I HAVE to come back. Just to see what you have up your sleeve." She hugged Angela and went home. She realized as she drove, that she wasn't nearly as nervous as she had been. Angela really had a way of taking the stress away.

The next night the girls spent their evening shrinking the pile of note cards down to a third of the size and reworking the remaining ones to go with the posters. To Mary Beth, it seemed as though she were doing all this work for someone else. The speech had slipped her mind as she worked with Angela.

On Thursday, the living room furniture had been rearranged to look like a classroom, with chairs lined up facing the front, where Angela had placed an easel. On all of the chairs but one was a stuffed animal. Mary Beth laughed.

"What? These are your classmates for the evening. I hand-picked them myself. They are all good listeners, I promise, and won't laugh at you if you fall over. I warned them that they would get sent to the principal if they did," Angela told her, trying hard to look serious.

Mary Beth gestured to the empty chair. "What about that one? Did he already misbehave?"

"Nope, that's where I get to sit," Angela replied. "I figured you needed at least one audience member who knew how to clap."

They practiced Mary Beth's speech several times before the doorbell rang. It startled Mary Beth and she ran out of the room. Angela opened the door. It was dinner, cooked and delivered by a local pizza place. Angela quickly took the pizza and paid the delivery boy. Mary Beth joined Angela in the kitchen. The girls took a break and ate stuffed crust pizza with sausage and onions. Mary Beth felt much more at ease with her speech. It was easy when the audience was so cute and fluffy.

By nine o'clock, Mary Beth was actually enjoying herself. Angela had the stuffed animals posing and clapping and calling 'encore!' They rolled on the floor laughing after one teddy bear did a backflip off its chair and knocked all the other animals onto the floor.

Thank you, Lord, for Angela. She is an amazing friend and I am so lucky that she is in my life.

Angela hugged Mary Beth tightly and told her how proud she was of the progress she had made. She told her that phase five was the final stage. It would take place the next night at the same time. Mary Beth was actually looking forward to what Angela had in store for her. She had a spring in her step as she left for home.

Five o'clock found Mary Beth on Angela's porch, ringing the doorbell. In her bag, she had a bottle of wine and she carried a cheese cake. It was the least she could do for all that Angela had done to help her with this fear. Besides, they needed to celebrate phase five. As she stood there, she could hear voices inside. Puzzled, she rang the bell again. It took several minutes before Angela answered the door. Her face was flushed and she was out of breath.

"All right, what's going on?" Mary Beth demanded. She used her most stern voice and put her one free hand on her hip.

"Nothing's going on," Angela insisted. "Are you ready for phase five?" She moved to the side and waved Mary Beth into the house.

The living room was set up the same way it had been the night before. The only difference that Mary Beth could spot was that all the doors leading off of the living room were closed. Normally they would be open. She handed Angela the cheesecake and the wine. They took them to the kitchen and put them in the refrigerator.

"How about we practice before dinner?" Angela suggested, trying to sound nonchalant.

They walked into the living room and Angela took her seat among the stuffed animals. They had all returned to their spots after the teddy bear kerfuffle from the night before. Mary Beth took her place at the front of the room. She gave her speech, using the easel to display her poster board points.

Angela clapped and cheered when she finished. "That was great! I loved it! But, I think I have something that will help you take this to the next level. Wait right there." She stood up and walked over to the door to the downstairs powder room. She opened the door and out walked Adam.

"What in the world?" Mary Beth cried. "What are you doing here?"

"I'm here for phase five," Adam said simply giving her a hug and taking a seat from a stuffed turtle and placing it in his lap.

"I thought you should have more clapping," Angela said and took her seat. "Go ahead and give it again."

Mary Beth took a deep breath and looked at Adam. Speaking in front of Angela had become easy. Adding Adam to the mix brought back some of her anxiety. She nervously shifted her weight from one foot to the other. Clearing her throat, she started her speech. She stumbled a couple of times but managed to make it through.

Adam stood up and clapped for her. "That was great! I am impressed! But I think that I have something that will help you. Hold on a second." He walked over to the spare bedroom and opened the door. Out came Grandma Rose.

Mary Beth laughed out loud. "Are you here for phase five, too?"

"Of course, I am!" Grandma Rose said, giving Mary Beth a big hug. "I want to see you succeed in this. Let's hear that speech!" She walked over to the couch and sat between the pink bunny and the black and white Dalmatian. She folded her hands and looked at Mary Beth expectantly. Adam and Angela took their seats, too. They all looked at Mary Beth and waited for her to begin.

Mary Beth smiled nervously at each one and tapped her cards on her hand. She looked down at her notes and realized that her hands weren't shaking. *That's an improvement. I think I can do this!* She started to speak and looked at each of her friends. She could sense their love for her and it boosted her confidence. Her voice gained strength and she stood up straighter. This time through, she didn't stumble once.

Amid the clapping, Grandma Rose walked up to Mary Beth and took her face in her hands. "That was wonderful, honey. I am so proud of you! But I think I have something that will help you do even better. Stay here for a minute." She walked to the bottom of the stairs and called, "You can come out now!"

Doors opened, and footsteps sounded in the hallway. One, two, three pairs of legs descended the steps. "Hello, Mary Beth," her dad said, coming into the room. Behind him came Mary Beth's mother and Angela's boyfriend, Craig. "We're part of phase five, whatever that means."

Mary Beth laughed and laughed. She grabbed Angela in a big bear hug. "You are insane! I love you!" She hugged her parents, and even Craig. Everyone settled into their seats, stuffed animals in their laps. "I see we have a full house, tonight!"

Smiling, she gave her speech one last time. She didn't feel nervous at all and spoke smoothly and confidently. Soon it was over and everyone cheered. Mary Beth took a bow. She had never felt better. She was sure that she would be able to deliver the speech to her class, no problem.

Surgery

November in Fort Collins was brown and cold. Business was booming. Mary Beth had scored a job with the city's parks and recreation. They needed help organizing all their summer equipment. Classes were going well. Mary Beth currently had all As. Her speech had gone without a hitch. Life was good.

Then, early one morning, Mary Beth woke up in terrible pain. She curled up in a ball and breathed through her mouth. She had never felt pain like this before. It centered in her middle back and seized her up completely. Then came the nausea. She crawled into her bathroom and threw up in the toilet. She lay on the floor panting. She was cold and clammy. The pain eased and she stood up. Rinsing out her mouth, she looked in the mirror. Her face was white as a sheet.

She climbed back in bed and fell asleep. Soon she was awake again, pain wracking her body. It kept getting worse and worse. She was drenched in sweat and panting for breath. She moaned and cried out. *God, what's wrong with me? I've never felt like this before. Please help me!*

She managed to find her phone in between episodes and called Adam. "Adam, I need you! Please help me!" she groaned as the pain gripped her again. She dropped the phone and curled up on the bed.

Soon, Adam showed up at the door. He pounded on it and called Mary Beth's name. There was no answer. He pounded again, called out again. Still nothing. He tried the doorknob. It was locked. Backing up, he raised his foot and smashed it against the lock. The jamb splintered and he pushed his way into the apartment. He rushed to the bedroom and found Mary Beth rocking back and forth and groaning on the bed.

"What's wrong?" he asked her.

She shook her head and threw up all over the comforter. Her breathing was fast and shallow. Her face was pale and her eyes were glazed over. He scooped her up in his powerful arms and carried her out through the broken door, down the hall, down the stairs, and swiftly put her into his car.

Mary Beth whimpered as the car sped through the predawn quiet to the hospital. Adam pulled up in front of the emergency room and raced around the car. He picked Mary Beth up as if she weighed nothing and carried her inside. A nurse rushed over and helped him put her into a wheelchair. They took her back to an examination room. Another nurse came over to Adam and asked him for some information about Mary Beth. He answered her swiftly and concisely as his training kicked in. The nurse disappeared into the examination room and left him alone.

Adam paced in the waiting room. He called Mary Beth's parents and woke them up. Next, he dialed Angela's number and told her what was going on. He sat down on a hard, orange chair. He couldn't sit still. Soon he was up and pacing again. He stopped at the nurse's station several times for an update, but they wouldn't tell him anything, since he wasn't a relative. He tried to sit again. *God, I don't know what is wrong, but please, please, watch over Mary Beth.*

Mary Beth was being poked and prodded at that moment by the emergency room doctor. He asked her about her symptoms and manipulated her organs. Mary Beth tried her best to remain still for the examination, but it was very hard for her. When the doctor finished looking her over, he left. Mary Beth stood up and paced around the room. She got some relief from the pain that way. She still had to hunch over as she walked, but at least it helped a little. A nurse came in and drew some of her blood. After she was gone, Mary Beth continued to pace. The isolation was starting to get to her. She missed Adam, she missed Angela, she wanted her mother.

As if on cue, the door opened and her parents stepped in. Mary Beth rushed to her mother and fell into her arms. Her dad grabbed them both. They stood like that for several minutes. Mary Beth started to cry. "Oh, Mom, Dad, thank you for coming! I hurt so bad and I don't know what's wrong. This is the worst pain I've ever felt in my life. It won't go away."

Mr. and Mrs. Gates took turns asking Mary Beth questions. Mrs. Gates kept touching Mary Beth. She rubbed her arm, stroked her hand, felt her forehead. Mary Beth let her. It felt good knowing that her parents were there and that they cared about her.

After an eternity, there was a knock on the door and the doctor returned. "I believe that we know what is causing the pain, Mary Beth," he said. "It looks as if you have kidney stones."

"What? Really?" Mary Beth said. "I thought you had to be older to get those. I'm only 26!'

"They can strike anyone, at any time. But, there are some risk factors that make some people more susceptible to them than others," the doctor continued. "For example, drinking a lot of sports drinks that contain minerals, not drinking enough water, family history, eating a lot of sugar and salt, these can all put you at risk for them."

He turned to Mary Beth's parents. "Have either of you ever had kidney stones?"

Both her parents shook their heads. "No one in our family has ever had one," Mrs. Gates said, shrugging her shoulders.

"Well, I'd like to send you to a urologist to have it checked out. They can help you decide on your options for dealing with the situation. In the meantime, I'm going to give you a shot that will give you some relief," the doctor said. He had Mary Beth turn around and expose her hip. Immediately she could taste the medicine in her mouth. The pain in her back went away at the same time.

"That stuff is amazing!" she exclaimed. "It's like flipping a switch. I hurt like crazy and, BAM! The pain's gone!"

"It's pretty powerful medicine. I can only give you one more of these. It can damage your liver if you have too much of it," the doctor warned. "So, make an appointment tomorrow with the specialist."

They thanked the doctor and walked out to the waiting room. Angela and Adam stood up quickly and came to meet them. They both had looks of concern on their faces. A group hug was called for immediately. Mary Beth told them about what had happened.

She looked around the group sheepishly. "Thank you for coming to the hospital in the middle of the night. I really appreciate the support. I'm sorry to have gotten you all out of bed."

After one more big hug from each of the special people in her life, Mary Beth allowed Adam to take her home. When they arrived, Mary Beth saw that her apartment door was open. Then she saw the broken door jamb. She looked at Adam with a frightened look on her face.

"Did someone break in while we were gone?" she asked in a horrified whisper.

"Nah. I did that," Adam admitted. "When I couldn't get you to answer the door, I kinda broke it in. Sorry about that. I'll fix it, but first, let's get you into bed." He ushered Mary Beth into her house and took her to the couch and made her lie down.

"Give me a minute to clean up the bedroom, then you can go to bed. You made a big mess in there before we left." He left her there and went in search of clean sheets and blankets. After a few minutes, he returned and helped her to her feet. She allowed herself to be escorted to her bed. It felt so nice to have Adam there, taking care of her.

She climbed in between the cool sheets with only a twinge of embarrassment as she remembered getting sick all over the other ones. She started drifting off to sleep, but was startled awake by a loud banging sound. "Adam?" she called out. "What was that?"

"Sorry, trying to hammer the pieces of your door back together. I'm almost done, then you can sleep." He had found her 'Do It Herself Kit' in the hall closet and was holding a hammer that had a pink handle.

Mary Beth giggled at the sight.

"What? Men can use pink hammers, too, you know," Adam said in mock irritation. He smiled at her and kissed her on her forehead. He left and continued banging on the wooden door frame. When he finished, he returned to the bedroom carrying a tall glass of ice water. "The doctor said you should try to drink more water." He helped her sit up in bed and take a long drink. He fluffed the pillows and tucked her in. "Nighty, night," he said and shut the door as he left.

A few hours later she awoke and stretched in the bed. At first, she was confused by the slant of the sunbeams across the floor. Then she remembered why she was still in bed. The pain was still gone, but the memory of it stayed with her. She climbed out of bed and padded her way to the bathroom. On her way, she could hear the TV. She went to the end of the hall and saw Adam on the couch.

"I thought you had left," she said simply.

Adam shook his head. "Not after the way you scared me last night. I thought someone should stick around and make sure you were

OK. I also called the urologist and made you an appointment for this afternoon."

"What time is it now?" Mary Beth asked, trying to smooth down her bed head.

"Eleven thirty. Appointment's at one. If you want a shower, I suggest you do it now," Adam said in his take charge voice.

"Yes, sir!" Mary Beth saluted and scooted into the bathroom before Adam could respond.

Half an hour later, Mary Beth emerged dressed in jeans and sweater. She felt better and was even hungry. She could smell food and followed her nose to the kitchen. Adam had made some tomato soup with grilled cheese sandwiches.

"Yummy!" Mary Beth exclaimed, "One of my favorites. I like this restaurant. Did you have to use a pink spatula to make it?" She shrieked when Adam tried to swat her with a dish towel. Adam served the lunch at the dining room table, where he had Mary Beth's laptop open.

"I did a little research on kidney stones while you were asleep," he said. "It sounds like they mostly pass out of the body on their own, but can be pretty painful while they do it. If they get to be too large, they might have to take them out surgically."

"Really?" Mary Beth looked green. "I can't stand the thought of going to sleep and putting my life in someone else's hands."

"Well, let's hope the doctor has good news for us, then," Adam said.

That afternoon, Adam accompanied Mary Beth the urologist's office. The first thing they had to do was take x-rays of her mid-section. Then, they waited for the doctor to study the images. After watching the clock slowly tick by fifteen minutes, they were called into his office. He had a large computer screen set up with her x-ray images.

"These white spots here are kidney stones," he said, using his computer mouse to circle the small, bright spots on the computer. He circled two on the left side and one on the right.

"I have more than one?" Mary Beth asked incredulously.

"You have at least three," the doctor confirmed. "I measured these and they are between .7 and .8 millimeters across."

"Is that good or bad?" Adam asked.

The doctor shook his head. "That's definitely not good. The ureter, the tube leading from your kidney to your bladder is about .5 millimeters. Stones as large as yours sometimes pass on their own, but most likely, it will require surgical intervention."

Mary Beth gripped Adam's hand until her knuckles turned white. "What can I do to make them pass on their own?"

"Drink lots of water," the doctor advised. "I will write you a prescription for some pain medication. The shot they gave you last night will wear off soon. I really don't think that you are going to be able to pass these on your own, but I could be wrong."

"I'd like to give it a try," Mary Beth said. "I'm not too keen on the idea of having surgery. It's definitely up there on the fear o meter."

She and Adam waited for the prescription and then went downstairs to the pharmacy to fill it. Mary Beth had been holding Adam's hand for the entire appointment. It was like a life line for her. She felt safer knowing he was with her. They went back to her apartment and sat on the couch. Adam brought Mary Beth her largest glass, filled to the brim with water. "Drink," he said, simply.

Mary Beth took a large gulp of water, then another. She was determined to do everything she could to pass this stone. The doctor had told her that it could take as little as a few hours, or as much as a week for the stone to come out. She was definitely rooting for the former.

The appointment had reassured Adam that Mary Beth wasn't in immediate danger, and he decided he should go to the home improvement store to get materials to do a permanent repair on Mary Beth's door. While he was gone, Mary Beth e-mailed her professors to explain her absence in class and ask for an extension on a paper that was due the next day. She also moved the sheets that Adam had washed to the dryer. She managed to drink another glass of water before he returned with his supplies.

The phone rang several times, her parents called to find out how she was feeling. Angela called, too, and promised to go to 7-11 to get her a Big Gulp cup. Even her sister, Melody, called to check on her.

"I guess I know what it takes to get attention around here," she smirked as she walked past him to the bathroom.

Adam frowned at her. "You scared everyone last night. You about gave me a heart attack!"

Mary Beth closed the door. She sat down and went, and went, and went. It felt like she had just lost a gallon of fluid. As she turned to flush, she noticed that the water wasn't the normal yellow. It was dark pink. The sight of it caused her stomach to do flip flops. *Oh, no! It's getting worse! God, help me!*

When she came back to the living room, Adam took one look at Mary Beth's ashen face and came running. He helped her sit down and asked, "What's wrong? Is the pain back?"

"No," Mary Beth whispered, "I feel fine, except now there's blood in my urine. Just like the urologist predicted." She leaned backward against the cushions and covered her face with her hands.

"I can't do this, Adam, I'm so scared! What if I go to sleep on the operating table and never wake up?" She was sobbing now. Adam sat beside her and gathered her in his arms.

"It'll be OK," he said, trying hard to think of the right words to say. "Lots of people have surgeries every day and are fine. There's nothing to worry about."

Mary Beth only cried harder. She couldn't do this. "I hate needles, I'm terrified of them. What if something goes wrong?"

Adam patted and rubbed her back. Gently he reminded her, "What is the alternative? Do you want to be in pain and have all this blood?"

"I just want it to go away," came her muffled reply. She had turned away from Adam and put her face in a pillow. Her shoulders started to shake with her sobs and Adam grabbed the tissue box from the end table.

He handed her a tissue and continued to rub her back. He was at a loss for words. Silently he prayed, *God, I don't know how to help Mary Beth. Please comfort her. Take away her fears and help her to make a wise decision here. Show me what to do to support her.*

After a while, the sobs grew quieter and the shaking stopped. Mary Beth sat up and blew her nose. She wiped her face and took a few deep breaths. A sob still escaped every now and then, but they were getting smaller and farther between. She turned back towards Adam and leaned on his shoulder. He wrapped his arm around her and they sat in silence until her breathing turned to normal.

"Sorry about the outburst," Mary Beth said softly. "I have a deathly fear of surgery, as if you couldn't tell."

"Nope, didn't notice," Adam returned, trying to make her smile. He didn't get the smile, but he did get one corner of her mouth to turn up. "All kidding aside, Mary Beth, I think you need to seriously consider it. From what the doctor said, those things are so large, they can't come out on their own. If you are seeing blood, that means they could be damaging your urinary tract. You could get an infection or something."

Mary Beth picked at her cuticles. "You're right. I just don't want to think about it right now. Could we watch a movie or something for a while? I want to just forget about all of this."

"Sure," Adam agreed. They settled on a cheesy comedy and spent the next hour and a half laughing.

The next morning, Mary Beth once again found blood in her urine. She continued to ignore it. She took her pain medication, but it didn't work as well as the shot she had gotten at the emergency room. She went about her day, trying to act as if nothing were wrong. She took the Big Gulp cup that Angela had brought her and filled it full of ice water. She set herself the goal of finishing it by noon.

It was hard for her to concentrate on her classes that morning. It was difficult to find a comfortable position in the hard, plastic chairs. She shifted in her seat and ended up sitting on the very edge, with her back very straight. It gave her little relief. Her second class was almost unbearable and by the third class she took to standing in the back of the room. She would rock from side to side, trying her hardest to look studious and pay attention.

She managed to drink all of her water and made it to her office at her normal time. She refilled the glass in the break room and took her medication. In the bathroom, the story was the same as it had been that morning. The afternoon passed even more slowly than the morning had. The medication seemed to wear off more quickly and the pain came back with an intensity she could barely stand. She left her last client early and went straight home. She propped herself on the couch and put a heating pad on her back.

God, I don't know how much more of this pain I can stand. Please, please, help me to pass these stones.

She picked up her phone and called Angela. "Can you come over tonight? I need some company. This kidney stone thing stinks." Angela agreed to come as soon as she closed shop and would bring dinner.

Mary Beth went to the bathroom and decided to take a hot bath, thinking that would give her some relief. She poured a copious amount of bubble bath into the water and climbed in. The water surrounded her aching body and soothed her frazzled brain. For a while she found that the pain lessened, but just when she was able to finally relax, it came roaring back. Groaning, she stood up and stepped out of the tub. She dried herself off and slipped into some flannel pajamas.

Just as she walked into the living room, there was a knock on the door. Opening it, a smile lit up her face. Not only was Angela there with a bag of groceries, but so was Adam. Moving to the side, she let them in, hugging each in turn.

"What a surprise! I thought you had to work tonight," she said to Adam.

"I traded shifts with a buddy. I figured you'd need some distraction tonight. Knowing you, I would guess that you pushed yourself to do your normal stuff today. Am I right?" Adam said.

Mary Beth dropped her head guiltily. "Yes, I did. I thought that if I kept busy, the pain would go away or I could ignore it. Didn't work, though. I'm feeling pretty lousy at the moment."

They made their way to the kitchen and unloaded the bags of groceries that Angela had brought. There was a rotisserie chicken, some rolls, potato salad, and a half gallon of ice cream. Everyone dished up their plates from the counter and then went to the table. Adam said the blessing, adding in an extra prayer for healing for Mary Beth.

"Thank you, Adam," Mary Beth said.

They ate and talked about their day. Mary Beth got up frequently to walk around the room. She took her medication and tried to focus on her friends.

"Why don't we try a massage?" Angela suggested. "Go lay on the couch. I'll get some lotion and rub your back."

"I'll clean up the kitchen while the masseuse gets to work," offered Adam. He picked up their plates and started to work.

Mary Beth was willing to try anything so she willingly went to the living room and lay face down on the couch. Angela found some lotion in the bathroom and rubbed it on her lower back. "Does that feel OK?" she asked.

Mary Beth nodded. Her eyes were closed and she was trying hard to relax. The back rub felt wonderful, but it couldn't quite reach the pain. It helped her back muscles to unclench, but that dull ache remained. The spike to intense pain continued to come and go, even with the help of the medicine and the nursing of her friend.

After a while, Mary Beth sat up. "Thank you, Angela, that was great. I think I need to walk around for a little while." She got up off the couch and started pacing the floor.

Watching her, Adam said, "Not any better, is it?"

Mary Beth said, "Not really. I can't seem to get comfortable at all. I even tried a hot bath. I drank at least a gallon of water today and it feels like I've peed twice that amount. Those stones should be coming out by now, shouldn't they?"

Adam reminded her that the doctor said it could take up to a week for the stones to pass.

Mary Beth cringed. "I don't think I can take a week of this. I can't sleep, I can't eat, I can't sit, I can't stand. This is miserable!"

Both Adam and Angela looked at her with sympathy. "I wish there was something more we could do to help you," Angela said.

"Me, too," Mary Beth sighed. "I think I'll try to get some sleep. The doctor said I could take some of that PM pain killer. I'll try that and see how it goes."

She hugged her friends as they left. Both Angela and Adam admonished Mary Beth to call them if she needed anything. She promised that she would.

It took a while for the sleep aid to kick in, but finally Mary Beth felt sleepy enough to go to bed. She was able to get a few hours' rest, but nothing completely took away the pain, so she tossed and turned.

The next morning, she was up early. The bedding was twisted into a giant mess and she finally gave up trying to get comfortable. She went into the bathroom and looked at herself in the mirror. Her reflection was pale and there were huge dark circles under her eyes. Her hair was standing at odd angles all over her head.

Mary Beth sat on the toilet and crossed her fingers. *Maybe it would be normal this morning*, she thought. No such luck. In fact, if she was honest, it looked a little bit worse. Gritting her teeth. She went to the kitchen and forced herself to drink a large glass of water. Suddenly a sharp pain gripped her and she gasped aloud. Grabbing the countertop, she leaned over and tried to keep breathing. The pain continued and Mary Beth dropped to her knees, feeling nauseous. Tears streamed down her cheeks. *Oh, God, please help me!*

When the pain eased a little, Mary Beth picked up the phone and called the urologist. Because it was so early, they weren't open yet, but an answering service did pick up the call. Mary Beth asked them, between breaths, to have the doctor call her as soon as he could. They promised to relay the message and hung up.

Mary Beth took the phone with her to the bathroom and filled the tub. She climbed into the hot water and slowly lay back. The pain had eased somewhat and she could at least think straight. *What am I going to do? I can't bear this pain for an entire week. I just can't! But surgery? No way! Not an option!*

The phone interrupted her thoughts. It was the doctor, returning her call. She quickly told him about the blood and the fact that the pain medication no longer worked. He told her to come to the office as soon as she could.

When she arrived at the doctor's office, she was ushered into the x-ray department. Then she waited for the doctor. Soon, he came out to get her himself. "Come with me," he said. "I need to show you something." They went to the same office they had before and there on the screen were the familiar pictures.

Taking the computer mouse, he moved the curser to the picture of her left kidney. "Look at your left kidney," he said. "Now look at your right one. Do you see how much larger the left one is? It wasn't that way before. Here's why." He moved the curser to the bottom portion of the screen. "Right here, where your ureter joins the kidney is your stone."

Mary Beth leaned in and saw a bright, white spot. She looked at the doctor. He was frowning.

"I measured it again, and this one is much larger than I originally thought. This one is .9 millimeters across. Remember, your ureter is about .5 millimeters. This stone is blocking the tube. All the fluid is backing up in the kidney. That's why it is larger than the other one. There is no way that you will be able to pass that stone on your own. We need to take it out."

Mary Beth blanched. She sat back in the chair and grabbed the arms. "I.... you... can't we... isn't there something else we can try?"

"From the way you described your symptoms and these pictures, the sooner we act, the better. It will only get worse if we wait. You could damage your kidney," he said gently.

Mary Beth mutely nodded. She didn't trust her voice right then. She was holding her breath, trying to keep from crying. This was her worst nightmare! Suddenly her resolve left her and her face crumpled. She burst into tears. The doctor reached for a tissue. He sat beside her and tried to soothe her. He explained that she would only be in the hospital one day, and that they wouldn't have to make any incisions. She would be at home, in her own bed that same night. His words reached her and his tone calmed her. "OK," she said in a very small voice. "When do we do this?"

"I have an opening tomorrow. Let's walk to the reception desk so you can get the details," the doctor replied. He put his arm around her shoulders and they walked out of the room and down the hall.

Mary Beth left the office with a packet of information and an appointment for 7 a.m. the next morning. She felt miserable, both physically and emotionally. She drove to her parents' house instead of going home. She didn't want to be alone just then, and wanted to talk to them about what was going on.

That night, Mary Beth called Angela and Adam and told them that she was scheduled for surgery the following morning. They both said they wanted to be there for her and agreed to meet her at the hospital. She spent the night in her childhood bedroom, unsuccessfully trying to get comfortable. Around 5 a.m., she finally gave up trying and went downstairs to the kitchen. She started to make some breakfast, then remembered she couldn't eat before surgery.

Sighing, she put the box of cereal back in the cupboard and the bowl back on the shelf. She wandered into the living room and stood looking out the window. *Lord, this is the biggest leap of faith yet. I am putting myself in someone else's hands and have no control over what happens. I want to trust you for the best outcome, but I'm afraid. Please help me to trust you with this.*

She went to her room and got dressed. When she went back downstairs, her mom was in the kitchen, sitting at the bar. Her head was bowed and her eyes were closed. Mary Beth stood quietly and watched her. It warmed her heart to see her mom talking to God. She smiled and sat down beside her. They clasped hands and Mrs. Gates continued her prayers, "Lord, thank you for my beautiful daughter. Today is going to be a difficult day for her. Please wrap her in your love and protection. Guide the surgeon's hands and give him the wisdom to do his job well. Keep Mary Beth safe and comfort her and calm her fears. In Jesus name, I pray, amen." She put her arms around her daughter and hugged her for a long time.

Soon Mary Beth and her parents arrived at the hospital to check in. As they walked into the outpatient surgery center, they saw Adam and Angela. They pulled Mary Beth into a bear hug. She was barely able to hold her emotions in check. Her breathing was shallow and she could barely make herself look above her shoes.

The nurse came to take her back to prep her for surgery. Her mom went with her. She changed into a hospital gown and placed all her street clothes into the bag they gave her. She lay on the bed and the nurse raised the end up so she was sitting up. After checking her blood pressure and pulse, another nurse had her sign the hospital forms.

Then they waited. Mary Beth's stomach was growling since she hadn't eaten anything. She wouldn't have been able to, even if she could have. Her nerves were raw with fear and she ached very badly. Her mom tried to make small talk to keep Mary Beth's mind off of what was coming. It didn't work very well.

"Have you seen Adam's grandma lately?" Mrs. Gates asked.

"Yes," Mary Beth said, picking at her cuticles, "I try to go over every week."

"That's nice. What is she up to these days?"

"She goes to the senior center and plays games. Sometimes they go places."

"Oh. Where do they go?"

"A movie, an art exhibit. One time they took a day trip to Rocky Mountain National Park."

"I love going there. Remember the hike we took to Alberta Falls the summer you were learning to drive?"

"Yes," Mary Beth said. Just then the nurse returned with some equipment. Mary Beth stiffened and her eyes got wide.

The nurse turned to her and said, "We're going to put in a pick line right now. Which arm do you want me to use?"

"What's a pick line," Mary Beth asked, eyeing the equipment.

"It's a needle with an attachment, so we only have to poke you once. We can use it for drawing blood, anesthesia, driplines, whatever we need."

"Oh, my left arm, I guess," Mary Beth said.

The nurse brought the stand around to the left side of the bed. She had Mary Beth hang her arm over the side and shake it. Then she prepped the needle. Mary Beth grabbed her mom's hand and squeezed it tight. She closed her eyes and held her breath. A sharp prick and a feeling like a hot poker hitting her skin moved up her arm.

"All done," the nurse said cheerfully. "The anesthesiologist should be here in a minute. You did great. This will all be over before you know it. You will feel so much better!" She patted Mary Beth on the shoulder and took her tray out of the room.

Mary Beth held onto her mom like a person drowning. Tears leaked out of her eyes and down her cheeks. Her hands were shaking and her heart was pounding. She wanted to get up and run away, but she knew she had to see this through.

"I'm scared, Mom," she whispered.

"I know, honey, so am I. Let's put this in God's hands, okay?" Mrs. Gates bowed her head and prayed over Mary Beth.

When she finished, they both opened their eyes and smiled at each other. Mary Beth's smile was a little wobbly, but she tried to look brave. *Lord, I trust you, I do, but this is so hard for me.*

The door opened and a man wearing blue scrubs walked in. "I'm your anesthesiologist," he said loudly. "We are ready to get started. I'm going to put some medicine in your pick line that will help you to relax." He inserted a needle and a cold sensation went up Mary Beth's arm. She immediately felt calmer and sleepy.

Mrs. Gates said good bye, gave Mary Beth a hug and went out the door.

"Now we'll give you something to make you sleep," the loud man said. "I want you to count backwards from ten to one."

Mary Beth made it to seven and the lights went out.

December

    The holiday lights around Fort Collins always put Mary Beth in a great mood. It was especially magical at night when snow was falling, like it was tonight. Mary Beth and Adam were walking hand in hand around Old Town, in the center of Fort Collins. They were Christmas shopping and having a wonderful time. Music was coming from hidden speakers, lights were twinkling, the mood was just right.

    They decided to stop and have some hot chocolate at one of the small restaurants. Sitting at a small table next to a roaring fireplace, they discussed their purchases and where they wanted to go next. When they had warmed themselves inside and out, they headed back into the cold night air.

    As they left the restaurant, they heard jingling bells. Turning to follow the sound, Mary Beth let out a small, "Oh!" There, coming down the street were two white horses pulling a beautiful black carriage. Sitting in the back was a man and a woman, obviously in love. Mary Beth stared after the horses and carriage as they went by. She was smiling.

    Turning to Adam she said, "Isn't that romantic?"

He smiled at her and watched the horses move away. "Very romantic," he said, grabbing her hand. "So is this." He put his other hand on the back of her neck and pulled her towards him. Their lips met for a long, slow kiss. Snowflakes landed on their faces, music played quietly in the background and the world disappeared.

The next two weeks were very busy for Mary Beth. She had finals in all of her classes, and with Christmas fast approaching, she was inundated with calls for help with organizing. She was surprised at this, but it seems that when people are expecting company for the holidays, they want their clutter to disappear.

With all the projects she had going, Mary Beth had limited time to organize her own life. She had lists of presents to buy, Christmas cards to write, parties to attend. Luckily her health had rebounded quickly after her surgery. It was amazing that something that small could wreak so much havoc on your life.

When Adam called to set up a dinner date the week before Christmas, she almost said no. She looked at her planner and panicked with all the appointments staring back at her. However, she knew she needed to spend time with her loved ones, so she rearranged her schedule to make room for him.

Saturday afternoon found Mary Beth deep in her closet, looking of just the right outfit. She wanted this date to be special. She planned to give Adam his present that night. She had found the perfect gift for him. It was an all-inclusive 3 day driving school put on at Pike's Peak International Speedway by Bob Bondurant. She couldn't wait to see the look on his face when he saw it. She knew that he had always dreamed of being a race car driver.

Finally, she found what she was looking for. A black woolen dress with red piping. It had long sleeves, a sweetheart neckline and a full skirt. It would go perfectly with her new leather boots. When Adam arrived to pick her up, she met him at the door with a sprig of mistletoe.

He didn't mind the tradition in the least. In fact, he made a mental note to stop under every piece of mistletoe he could find that night.

They drove slowly towards Old Town because the snow had begun to fall. It made for a beautiful scene with all the Christmas lights twinkling, but made for tricky driving conditions. Adam parked the car in a residential neighborhood, got out, and went around to hold the door for Mary Beth. She stepped out of the car, confused.

"Why are we parking here?" she asked. "Where are we going for dinner?"

"I had to park here because there aren't very many spaces by the restaurant. It's not a very long walk. Besides, I kind of like walking in the snow with you," Adam replied, taking her hand.

The two walked down the block and crossed the street. A few minutes later, Adam stopped in front of an unassuming building. The brick front had a black awning over the door. The name of the restaurant was obscured by the snow, but Mary Beth recognized one of her favorite places, Decadence.

"Oh, Adam, I love this place! How did you know?" Mary Beth exclaimed. She leaned up to give him a peck on the cheek.

Adam smiled down at her and held the door open. They entered the dark lobby and walked to the desk. A young woman wearing a dark top and black skirt looked at her reservation book and then took the couple to the dining room. She led them through the maze of tables and then around a corner. There, she escorted them to a private booth that was intimate and secluded. On the small table was a bouquet of red roses. "Enjoy," she said, leaving them with their menus.

Mary Beth exclaimed over the beautiful flowers. Adam was again rewarded with a kiss. They discussed the menu, picked their entrees, and ordered their meal. Light banter filled the evening as the two shared their food and they laughed at each other's attempts to eat the dessert portion without getting chocolate all over.

They lingered over the meal, enjoying every morsel. Finally, though, Adam checked his watch and asked Mary Beth if she were ready to leave. Agreeing that she was stuffed, they gathered their coats and the flowers and left their table. They paused at the door to don their coats. Then Adam opened the door and they stepped out into the cold. The snow was still falling gently. When Mary Beth looked up from zipping her coat, she froze.

There, in front of the restaurant, was a horse drawn carriage. The driver, dressed in a top hat with a sprig of holly and a long black overcoat, was standing next to the carriage, holding open the small door. He gestured to Mary Beth to enter. She turned and looked at Adam. He took her arm and led her over and helped her to step up onto the padded seat. He climbed in next to her and adjusted the plush red blanket around their knees.

The driver stepped up to the high seat at the front and snapped the reins. They moved smoothly down the street. Mary Beth, who was speechless, turned to Adam with big eyes.

"When did...how did... you... I've always wanted to ride in one of these. How did you know?"

"Lucky guess," Adam said with a twinkle in his eye. He put his arm around Mary Beth and pulled her closer.

"This is beautiful, Adam, thank you so much," Mary Beth said. "This would be the perfect time for you to open your Christmas gift." She pulled the envelope out of her pocket and handed it to him.

"What's this?" Adam asked.

"Open it and see," Mary Beth told him.

He carefully broke the seal and pulled out the papers inside. His jaw dropped as he read the contents. "Wow! This is great! I've always wanted to go to one of these schools!" He folded the papers and put them back into the envelope. Turning to her, he put his hands on either side of her face. He kissed her gently on each cheek followed by a long, passionate kiss.

When they finally came up for air, Adam said, "Now it's my turn." He reached into his coat pocket and produced a small velvet box. Opening it, he said, "Mary Beth Gates, would you take a leap of faith and marry me?"

Mary Beth's eyes grew wide and round. She looked at the box, looked at Adam, and opened her mouth to speak, but nothing came out. She watched Adam take the ring out of the box and she silently held out her hand. He slid the ring onto her finger as he watched her face.

"Mary Beth, will you?" he repeated softly. "I want to spend the rest of my life with you, taking leaps of faith together."

Finally finding her voice, Mary Beth whispered, "Oh, Adam! Yes! Yes! I would love to marry you!" She threw her arms around his neck and laughed. His arms wrapped around her and he pulled her onto his lap. Their lips found each other and they stayed that way for an eternity. When the carriage stopped, they pulled apart and looked around. They were back in front of Decadence. Slowly, they climbed down from the carriage and thanked the driver.

"Congratulations," he said, tipping his hat before climbing back up and driving away.

Mary Beth and Adam looked at each other shyly and held hands. They walked slowly back towards Adam's car, not wanting the evening to end.

"Can we stop at Grandma's Rose's house and tell her the good news?" Mary Beth asked. They were waiting for the car to warm up. She held her hand in front of her and studied the ring. It was a platinum setting with three stones. A large round diamond sat in the middle with a smaller diamond on each side. "It's beautiful, Adam. Thank you."

"Your welcome. I like the idea of telling Grandma Rose first, since she's the reason that we met in the first place." He put the car in reverse and backed out of the parking space. They drove slowly through the icy streets to the quiet street where Grandma Rose lived. Her house looked very festive with a large wreath on the door and colored lights strung along the eves. They parked the car and strolled up the walkway, hand in hand.

They rang the doorbell and waited. They could hear Christmas music playing inside and smelled cookies. The door opened and Grandma smiled when she saw who it was. "Come in, come in!" she said, opening the door wide and stepping to the side.

Both Adam and Mary Beth inhaled the scent of freshly baked sugar cookies as they stepped across the threshold. They followed Grandma Rose to the kitchen where the counters were covered with cooling cookies.

"The church is having a cookie exchange tomorrow. I wanted to make sure I had enough," Grandma Rose said, taking a plate out of the cupboard and placing cookies on it. She motioned for her guests to sit at the table and put the plate in the middle. "Please help yourself," she said. She poured them each a glass of milk and sat at the table with them. They munched on the delicious, warm cookies and talked about their week.

Adam cleared his throat and said, "Grandma, Mary Beth and I have something to tell you."

"You do? Something good, I hope," she said, smiling.

"We're getting married!" Mary Beth said, holding her hand out so Grandma Rose could see the ring. She could barely sit still, she was so excited.

Grandma Rose beamed as she inspected the ring. "I knew it! I knew you two were right for each other! I've been praying for this to happen." She stood and hugged the newly engaged couple. She wanted to know all about the proposal, which Mary Beth was more than happy to talk about. Poor Adam couldn't get a word in edgewise, but he didn't mind. He just sat and ate cookies and smiled at his two favorite women.

They helped Grandma Rose finish the last of her baking and packed them into containers for her party the next day. They said goodnight and headed out into the dark, cold starlit night. Their breath came out in clouds as they walked to the car.

They decided to tell their parents next. Since it was Christmas week, they planned to wait until the day after Christmas, when life would slow down a little. They rented out the back room at The Chicken and the Egg, and invited their families to meet them there for brunch. They invited Angela and Craig, too. Adam didn't tell his parents that Mary Beth's family were coming, and Mary Beth didn't tell her family that Adam's parents were going to be there.

As the families showed up, there was mass confusion as everyone was introduced to everyone else. Finally, the whole group managed to find seats at the long table. Adam stood up and got everyone's attention by clinking his knife against a glass.

"We invited you all here to help us celebrate. Mary Beth and I have decided to get married!" Mary Beth stood by his side, blushing. Adam put his arm around her and hugged her to his side. The room erupted in cheers. Everyone started talking at once, asking questions and trying to be the first to hug the new couple.

It took a long time for the room to get quiet again. The only thing that stopped the conversation was the waitress arriving to take orders. The second she left, the noise started again. Mary Beth and Adam beamed at each other. This was happy chaos.

When the food arrived, the noise level abated a little, but not much. They told everyone about the romantic proposal, which garnered Adam proud looks from his parents and approval from Mary Beth's. Mary Beth had to walk around the table so that everyone could get a look at the ring.

Even Mary Beth's sister, Melody, was on her best behavior. Not once did she try to tell a story about her engagement or compare her ring to Mary Beth's. She was polite and suitably impressed with her sister's fiancé. Mary Beth chalked her good behavior up to the fact that her kids took most of her attention, so she couldn't focus on ruining the event.

They were asked about their wedding plans. Adam looked at Mary Beth and said, "We haven't gotten that far yet. This is all brand new. We just found out about the engagement ourselves." Everyone laughed at this and offered suggestions for locations and dates. Mary Beth started to feel overwhelmed by all the details and ideas being thrown around. She began to pick at her cuticles, but Adam took her hand. She looked up at him and he frowned and shook his head.

"You don't need to stress about this, we'll figure it out together," he whispered.

She smiled and nodded. *I am so lucky to have such a wonderful man in my life,* she thought to herself. She looked around the table at the two families. She felt love swell her heart.

Ice

"How are the wedding plans going?" Angela asked between bites of cinnamon roll.

It was Saturday and the girls were sitting at their customary table in Café on Main. The smell of coffee and the sounds of muted conversations wafted around them.

"Everything is going fine, right now," Mary Beth said. "We don't want to have a huge wedding. We'd rather have a huge party. It seems like you do all this planning and spend all this money, and things get so stressful that you don't enjoy it. Our plan is to keep it simple and small. Then, when we get back from the honeymoon, we'll have a big party and invite all our friends."

Angela nodded. "I think that's a great idea! It can be less formal that way. Have you set a date, yet?"

"Not yet. We want a long engagement, especially since we haven't known each other very long. We want to do some pre-marital counseling first, so we can make sure our marriage starts off on the right foot," Mary Beth said. "You know, talk about finances, get on the same page about how we handle things, understand what bothers each of us, stuff like that. I'd rather figure that out now, than have fights about it later."

"You are so smart, Miss Organization," Angela said, looking at her friend with pride. "You are such a different person than you were a year ago. Remember what a mess you were?"

Mary Beth laughed. "I know, right? I had a rough start to my year, that's for sure. I was a total basket case!" She drank her hot chocolate and sighed. "The whole notion of taking a leap of faith completely altered the direction of my life. I can just imagine where I would be if we hadn't decided to do that. I never would have met Adam, that's for sure. Or Grandma Rose, either. I'd probably be working at another dead-end job instead of owning my own company. For sure I wouldn't be in graduate school right now."

"Wow, you're right. Taking a leap of faith was the best thing you could have done. You spent your Leap Year well, my friend," Angela said, raising her glass to Mary Beth.

"It's made me a stronger person, too. I kind of consider it my philosophy on life now," Mary Beth said, smiling. "You never know what will happen until you take a leap of faith. I'm not saying that it was easy by any means! Some of them were the toughest decisions I've ever made, but I'm glad I did. My faith in God has increased so much and I feel like my relationship with Christ is so much closer now. I can really see how He is working in my life."

Angela agreed, "I think you are so much more mature and centered. You don't have as many stressful days as you used to. Let me see your hands."

Mary Beth laid her hands on the table. Her cuticles were pink and health, not a rip or scab to be seen. "Adam has been helpful in that arena, too. He stops me every time he sees me start to pick. I don't feel like I carry as much stress when he's around, either. He calms me down."

"That's exactly how I feel about Craig," Angela said. "When you find the right person, life gets so much easier."

The girls bundled up and headed out into the cold, February day. They walked to Angela's store and went inside. Mary Beth looked around the cozy space. There were beautiful antiques of every shape and size. Large pieces of furniture were placed around the space and smaller pieces were displayed artfully. "You have done amazingly well, yourself, this year," she said appreciatively. She wandered around, picking up a few pieces and admiring them.

"Thanks, I appreciate that. You know I wouldn't be here if it weren't for you. Seeing you take leaps of faith really inspired me to look at my life, too. I am so happy with the way things have turned out. I can't wait to see what happens this year," Angela said.

"Me, too! Although it can be a scary thought, too. Taking leaps of faith isn't always the most comfortable situation to put yourself in," Mary Beth said, shuddering. She thought back to her kidney stone surgery. "Anyway, while I'm here, could you help me pick out a gift for Grandma Rose? Her birthday is coming up and I want to get her something special."

The girls browsed and discussed several items before settling on an art deco ring. It had a blue sapphire that matched the color of Grandma Rose's eyes. After wrapping up the ring, the girls left the store and locked up. They drove down to Washburn Shopping Center in Loveland to meet Adam and Craig. They had all agreed to go ice skating and then have lunch at Caliente, their favorite Mexican food restaurant.

"How was your drive?" Adam asked when they arrived.

"I-25 was pretty icy. We had to take it super slow in a couple of spots. It's so irritating that people are in such a hurry. I don't know how many times I got honked at," Mary Beth replied.

The group stopped at the kiosk and paid for ice skate rentals. They made their way to the stone wall next to the rink. A big fire was burning in the middle of the circular wall. Music blared from speakers around the rink. There were a few people skating, but mostly people were watching or warming themselves by the fire.

They made their way to the stairs. Adam helped Mary Beth climb up to the edge of the ice. They stepped out and started gliding around the rink. Mary Beth had always loved skating. She enjoyed the feeling of speed under her own power. It was fun moving in time to the music.

"You're pretty good at this, aren't you?" Adam asked, trying to keep up with her.

Mary Beth giggled. "Don't you skate much?"

"Hockey is more my thing than figure skating," he said. He took her hand and slowed her down. "That's better." They moved smoothly around the rink several times.

"Where are Craig and Angela?" Mary Beth asked, looking around. She had been so caught up in the moment, being close to Adam, that she had forgotten about her friend. She caught sight of the couple by the stairs. Craig was holding onto the rail for dear life and Angela was trying to wrangle him by one arm. They were both laughing hysterically.

Adam and Mary Beth made their way over. "What's going on here?"

Angela looked up, and between gales of laughter managed to say, "Craig thought he was a natural, but the second his skate hit the ice, he landed on his keister! Now he can't stand up at all!"

Craig's feet were at awkward angles to each other and he gritted his teeth. "I can do this. I just need to..." He tried again to stand up, but ended up on his face. This time Adam and Mary Beth joined the laughter. Adam grabbed one of Craig's arms, and Angela grabbed the other.

"One, two, three!" they shouted. Craig put his feet under himself and straightened his legs. He stood with his arms outstretched and wobbled back and forth, but he stayed standing. He attempted to take a step and almost lost his balance again. He grabbed the railing for dear life. Adam and Angela reached for him again. This time he managed to take several steps before he had to grab the side.

"I think I'm getting the hang of this. It's definitely a lot harder than it looks," Craig said, taking a few more tentative steps. Angela took his arm and showed him how to push off with one foot and glide. This helped him gain some momentum and soon the two of them were able to move together across the ice.

Adam took Mary Beth's hand and they headed around the rink again. They skated in companionable silence for several minutes. Then they noticed that Craig and Angela were sitting around the fire. They decided to join them and warm up.

Craig said, "My backside hurts. I think I'm done." He looked apologetically at Angela, who leaned over and kissed him.

"That's ok," she said. "I'm proud of you for trying. Skating isn't as easy as it looks."

Adam took a seat next to Craig. "We'll sit and watch if you girls want to keep skating."

Mary Beth looked at Angela, who shrugged her shoulders. "Maybe just a few more minutes, then." And they penguin walked over to the stairs.

Mary Beth and Angela took a few laps together, then Mary Beth decided to try some fancy moves. She skated backwards and did a few spins. Hearing cheering, she stopped and looked around. The boys had changed into their street shoes and were standing on the stone wall clapping. Adam did a wolf whistle, which made her blush. She curtsied and skated over to the edge.

Embarrassed, she made her way to the exit and over to the wall. She took off her skates and put on her shoes. Angela came and joined her. "Don't quit because of them! You are so beautiful to watch."

"Thanks, I guess I just got self-conscious. Let's go have some lunch. I'm starving!" Mary Beth said. She gathered her skates and walked to the kiosk. She didn't like being the center of attention. The others followed her and turned in their skates, too.

Snow was beginning to fall as they climbed into their cars and made their way to Caliente. After ordering, conversation turned to the wedding. Angela peppered the couple with questions about location, colors, flowers, and time.

Most of her questions were answered with, 'We don't know yet,' or 'We're still working on that.' They had decided to wait at least a year, but weren't sure if they wanted a summer wedding or a winter one. Adam and Mary Beth listened patiently to all of Angela's ideas and even Craig threw in an opinion or two.

Their food arrived, and conversation was forgotten as the hungry skaters dug into their enchiladas, burritos and tacos. They lingered over the last few bites, enjoying the company as much as the food. Finally, though, they reluctantly left the table.

Stepping out of the restaurant, they found that the snow storm had grown worse. The wind had picked up and started drifting the snow across the parking lot. Mary Beth dreaded driving in this kind of weather. "Would you mind driving me home?" she asked Adam. "I hate driving in storms."

Adam took her keys and turned to Craig and Angela. "Thanks for a fun day, drive safe," he said, shaking hands with Craig and hugging Angela. Mary Beth hugged them both and promised to call Angela the next day. They watched their friends climb into Craig's SUV and drive off. Then the hopped in the Mini Cooper and followed their tracks to the road.

Getting onto the interstate, the little car bucked and slid before settling into the tracks made by passing cars. Traffic was moving slowly and visibility was very low. Adam kept both hands on the wheel and concentrated on keeping the car on the road.

Suddenly, he took a sharp intake of air and stiffened. He moved the car as far to the right as he could without leaving his lane. He kept glancing in the rear view mirror every few seconds. Mary Beth asked, "What's wrong?"

Just then a giant semi-truck pulling a box trailer roared past, spraying snow all over them. The Mini Cooper rocked and slid. Adam fought the steering wheel to keep it straight. Mary Beth's heart was in her throat and she gripped the door handle hard. Adam managed to get the car under control after a few seconds. "That idiot! How can he possibly think it is safe to drive like that on roads like these?!" Adam's face was red, and he clenched his teeth.

They continued down the road for a few minutes, and then they saw red tail lights everywhere. The traffic came to a standstill and they saw people ahead of them getting out of their cars and running forward. "What's going on?" Mary Beth asked, straining to get a better look through the windshield.

"I don't know, but it can't be good," Adam said. "Stay here. I'm going to check it out. He left the car running and the heater on high. He zipped his coat up to his neck and pulled his ski cap further over his ears. When he opened the door, the snow swirled into the car. Mary Beth watched as he slipped and slid his way towards the front of the stopped cars. He disappeared into the storm and Mary Beth suddenly felt very alone.

Soon, she could hear sirens, then red and blue lights appeared in the whiteness. A state patrol SUV came by on the shoulder of the road followed by a fire truck and an ambulance. Mary Beth's eyes grew big and her heart started to beat harder. *Lord, there's been an accident. Please watch over whoever was involved, keep them in your hands. Give the rescue people the wisdom and knowledge to do what is needed for a good outcome.*

She continued to pray; it was the only thing she could do, sitting in the car, feeling lonely and clueless about what was going on. More emergency vehicles went by. She began to worry about Adam, out in the cold, but knew that because he was a police officer, he would probably be in the thick of the rescue that she imagined was happening.

After what felt like an eternity, Adam's form came through the snow. His coat was white and stiff with ice. His face was red and the look on his face was grim. He opened the car door and sat down.

"Is everything ok?" Mary Beth asked.

Adam just stared out the window and shook his head. He rubbed his hands together and flexed his fingers. With the heater going full blast, the ice began to melt on his hat and run down the sides of his face. He wiped the water from his face and turned to Mary Beth. He looked her in the eyes and said, "Craig and Angela were involved in the accident."

Mary Beth covered her mouth with her hands. Her eyes grew huge and the color drained from her face. "Are they ok?" she whispered. Her voice caught on the lump in her throat, making it hard for her to speak.

Again, Adam shook his head. "Mary Beth, they are taking them to Rocky Mountain Hospital. They are both in very bad shape. As soon as the traffic starts moving we can go there." He didn't say anything else, and Mary Beth didn't either. Adam took her hand and lifted it to his lips. Tears were running down his face and Mary Beth began to cry, too. *Oh, God, please watch over Craig and Angela,* she prayed silently.

Surround them with your love and protection. Guide the hands of the emergency people. Help them to save our friends!

Very slowly, cars in front of them began to move. Adam put the car in gear and pulled forward. Off to the side of the road, she could see Craig's SUV on its roof. The windshield was cracked and the side windows were broken out. The snow was churned up and mixed with dirt and sand all around the vehicle. The same semi-truck that had sped past them was lying on its side a little way past the battered SUV. Mary Beth stared at the scene as they drove past and they made their way up the interstate to RMH. They wound around to the emergency department and found a parking spot. Neither of them spoke a word the entire trip. They got out of the car and walked hand in hand to the door.

Once inside, Adam went to the information desk while Mary Beth called Angela's parents to tell them what she knew. She didn't know Craig's family's number, so she asked Angela's family to call them. As Mary Beth ended the call, Adam walked back to her. She looked questioningly at him.

"They have Angela in surgery right now," he said. "That's all they'll tell me. Craig is in the ICU."

They walked over to the waiting area and sat down. Mary Beth was shaking. Adam wrapped his arms around her and held her close. They sat like that for a long while. They watched people coming and going through the doors to the emergency room. Time seemed to slow and finally stand still. Mary Beth began to chew on her cuticles. Adam took her hands and held them in his.

The outside door opened, and Angela's mother came in. She rushed to the counter and started talking to the nurse. Mary Beth and Adam quickly crossed the room and joined her. When Angela's mom saw her, she cried out and enveloped her in a big hug.

"What's going on?" Mrs. Radcliffe asked, through her tears.

"They won't tell us anything, since we aren't family," Adam told her.

Mrs. Radcliffe turned to the nurse at the desk. "I am Angela Radcliffe' mother. Could you please tell me what is going on with her? Where is she? Can I see her?"

"Your daughter is currently in surgery. I will inform the doctor that you are here. Please have a seat," the nurse said, politely.

After thanking the nurse, the group made their way to the chairs that were arranged to look like someone's living room, complete with a coffee table and lamps. They all sat down and Adam told them about the accident.

"The roads, as you know, are in horrible shape. Craig was driving very cautiously. However, the person driving the semi wasn't. The semi got out of control and started slipping sideways. He crashed into the back of Craig's SUV, causing it to spin. They hit the embankment and flipped. The semi rolled over the top of them," Adam said. Mrs. Radcliffe was crying softly. Mary Beth had her arms around her.

"The top of the car was crushed, trapping both Craig and Angela inside. The firefighters had to use the jaws of life to cut the car to get them out," Adam blew his breath out and looked at his feet. He looked at Mrs. Radcliffe and Mary Beth, unsure if he should continue or not. Mrs. Radcliffe was rocking back and forth, sobbing quietly. Mary Beth was biting her lip, her face pale.

He decided not to share any more information until they heard from the doctor. He did what he could to comfort Angela's mother, while they waited for news. Craig's family joined them, and after introductions, they all sat quietly with their thoughts. The magazines on the coffee table were thumbed through and discarded. Small talk was out of the question. There was only one topic on everyone's mind, and there was no new information to discuss.

The doctor finally came out to talk to Mrs. Radcliffe. He was still wearing his scrubs from surgery. His hair and shoes were covered with blue disposable coverings. His blond, curly hair was peeking out from under the cap. He walked over to the group and asked, "Which of you is Angela's mother?"

Mrs. Radcliffe was on her feet before he finished talking. "I am Mrs. Radcliffe," she said in a rush. "How is Angela? Can I see her?"

"I'm Doctor Williams. Angela is now in the ICU. The car accident crushed her pelvis. She sustained severe internal damage, and we had to do extensive repairs to stop the bleeding. She has swelling in her brain, as well, and we have her in a drug induced coma at the moment," he said. "You can visit her for a few moments, but she will not know you are there."

Craig's father spoke up. "Excuse, me. Do you have any information about my son, Craig? He and Angela were together in the car accident."

"I don't have any information about your son. I will check with the nurse about who his physician is," Dr. Williams told him.

The two families followed him over to the desk. The doctor talked to the nurse who typed a few keys on her keyboard. "Craig's being taken care of by Dr. Kendall. I will have him paged for you." He turned to the nurse, who nodded and picked up the phone. "Now, Mrs. Radcliffe, please follow me." They walked through the set of double doors and disappeared.

Adam, Mary Beth, and Craig's parents wandered back to their spots on the couch to resume the wait for information. Knowing that Angela was in the ICU made them feel better in some ways, and worse in others. *Thank you for protecting her life and helping the doctor save her. She is in critical condition, Lord. Please, take away the swelling and heal her injuries.*

Mr. and Mrs. Samuelson held hands and prayed silently for their son. There were no more words to be said. Nothing could ease the pain of not knowing what was happening behind those big, black doors. Everyone was hoping for the best, but fearing the worst.

About a half an hour later, another doctor appeared. He looked tired and harried. His gray hair was standing on end and the stubble on his chin had gone past the 5 o'clock shadow stage. As he approached the group, the Samuelson's stood up to meet him. Mrs. Samuelson grabbed her husband by the arm.

"Mr. and Mrs. Samuelson? I'm Dr. Kendall. I've been taking care of Craig since they brought him in. Let's go somewhere private to talk," he said in a low voice. He walked off and the Samuelsons followed him, leaving Mary Beth and Adam alone.

They looked at each other. Neither one wanted to leave, but they didn't know what to do, or how long it would be before they received any word about their friends. They decided to wait for another hour, and then, if they didn't hear from anyone by then, they would drive home. The storm had let up and the sun was shining, so they felt safe waiting to drive the rest of the way to Fort Collins.

After another fifteen minutes, the double doors opened and Angela's mom came out. Mary Beth was instantly on her feet. Adam joined her and stood behind her with his hands on her shoulders. At first, Mrs. Radcliffe didn't see them, because she was crying so hard. She tried to get control of herself, but when she looked up, she saw Mary Beth and burst into tears again. Mary Beth rushed over to her and helped her to a seat.

Slowly, she told them what she knew. Angela was unresponsive due to the drug induced coma. She had tubes in her throat, wires monitoring her heart, needles in her arms. The surgeon had pinned her pelvis back together with an external fixator, which looked like a handlebar sticking out of her flesh.

"At least she can't feel the pain right now," Mrs. Radcliffe said, looking for a silver lining. "They will keep her in ICU until she is no longer critical, but they don't know how long that will be."

Adam and Mary Beth hugged her and asked if she needed anything. Mrs. Radcliffe said, "No, there is nothing we need right now, so I am going to go home and tell the family. They won't let me stay with her, there's not much room with all the machines. I'll be back tomorrow, if you want to join me."

They helped her to her feet and promised to see her the next day.

"Oh, I have added you two to the list of approved visitors, so you can go in and see her, just one at a time," she said before she walked outside.

Mary Beth immediately crossed to the desk and asked the way to the ICU. The nurse gave them directions in a curt, overworked voice and turned back to her computer. Not wasting any time, Adam and Mary Beth gathered their coats and hurried down the hall.

Turning the Tables

Mary Beth made her way up to the fifth floor of Rocky Mountain Hospital. She entered the Rehab Unit and said hello to the charge nurse at the front desk.

"Any change today?" she asked. The nurse frowned and shook her head.

Mary Beth sighed and made her way down the hall. She stopped at the third door and knocked. There was no answer.

Inside, she found Angela lying in the bed, surrounded by vases of flowers and balloons. She was staring out the window, unblinking. Her face was drawn and pale. Her blond hair was in a messy bun on top of her head. Her hands lay limp in her lap. It was the same every day. Angela had been in the rehab unit for two weeks and she refused to work at getting better.

Angela had been in a coma for three days after the accident. The swelling in her brain had gone down quickly and the doctors had moved her out of the ICU. She was healing well from her internal injuries, but she still sported the shiny metal bar that held her pelvis together while it healed.

She was mending well and after a week on the surgical ward, she had been moved upstairs to begin her physical therapy. It was at that point that she had begun asking questions about the accident.

Mary Beth looked at her friend, looking so frail and small in the white bed. Every time she walked into this room, her mind went back to that first day on the unit. Mary Beth, along with Adam and Mrs. Radcliffe had arrived with arms filled with flowers and balloons to brighten up the room.

Angela had looked at her mother and asked, "Mom, where is Craig? Is he here in the hospital, too? I want to see him."

Mrs. Radcliffe had smoothed the covers around Angela's shoulders, then looked her in the eyes and gently said, "Craig didn't make it, honey. He's gone."

"Gone? Gone where? Why hasn't he come to see me?" Angela furrowed her brow. She turned to Mary Beth. "Have you seen Craig? Did he get hurt, too?"

Tears rolled down Mary Beth's cheeks. She stood at the foot of the bed and said, "Angela, Craig is dead. He died after they brought him to the hospital. They tried to save him, but his injuries were just too great."

Angela had looked at her, looked at her mother, looked back at Mary Beth, then turned and stared out the window. Tears flowed from her eyes. Her expression went blank and she hadn't spoken a word since.

Today was no different. Angela was still looking out the window, but her eyes were dry. Mary Beth moved around the bed so that she was in Angela's line of sight. She began talking to Angela about her day. While she spoke, she picked up the hairbrush that was lying on the bedside table. She took out the hair tie and gently brushed all the knots out of her hair. When it was smooth and silky, she began styling it.

Suddenly, Angela caught her arm and pulled Mary Beth down to the bed. Mary Beth almost lost her balance, but caught herself and sat down next to her best friend. Angela had dark circles under her eyes. She searched Mary Beth's face, as if trying to figure out who she was. Her mouth moved, but no words came out.

Mary Beth said, "What is it, Angela? It's me, Mary Beth. Talk to me!"

In a whisper, Angela said, "Is it true? I had a dream that Craig died. Tell me that it was a dream, Mary Beth." She started breathing hard. She squeezed Mary Beth's arm and refused to let go.

Mary Beth spoke softly, trying to ignore the lump in her throat. "I am so sorry, Angela. It wasn't a dream. Craig didn't survive."

Angela sat quietly, searching Mary Beth's face. Then she nodded slowly, "I was afraid of that." Her face crumpled, and she began to sob. "Why? Why?" she cried.

Mary Beth held her and tried to soothe her. She explained what had happened; how the semi had sideswiped them and rolled over them on the ice, crushing the top of the car. She told her about the firefighters and how they had pried the car apart to get to her and Craig. She explained about her injuries and the coma. Angela cried through the whole thing. Finally, she began to calm down. Mary Beth continued to talk to her, telling her how the doctors had put her back together like a puzzle and gave her a suitcase handle across her pelvis.

It was as if Angela were truly waking up from a dream. Nothing had seemed real, she had been floating on the edge of consciousness. She looked around the room as if seeing it for the first time. "Where am I, now?" she asked.

"This is the rehabilitation unit at Rocky Mountain Hospital. You have been here for the past two weeks. The physical therapists have been here twice a day, every day, manipulating your limbs and trying to get you strong again. You haven't been the best patient," Mary Beth told her.

Angela said, "The last thing I remember was ice skating at Washburn Shopping Center and laughing at Craig because he couldn't stand up." A small smile played around her lips.

"That's right," Mary Beth told her. "We had gone skating that morning with the boys, then went to Caliente for lunch. The accident happened on the way home that day."

Just then, the nurse came in to take Angela's vitals. She paused just inside the door. "I thought I heard voices in here. Is Angela talking to you?" she asked Mary Beth.

Mary Beth nodded and smiled. "We've been talking about the accident. She doesn't remember anything about it. It was like a light switch turned on in her head and she came back to us!"

The nurse hurried to the bedside and checked Angela over. "The doctor will want to see her right away," she said and left to call him.

"What's the big deal?" Angela mumbled.

"You're kidding! You've been like a zombie for two weeks. Of course it's a big deal! You are acting like yourself again!" Mary Beth carefully hugged her friend. "I am so glad to see those bright eyes of yours and hear your sweet voice. Wait 'til your mom finds out!"

The doctor arrived to examine Angela, and Mary Beth stepped into the hall to make some phone calls. There were a lot of people praying for Angela and they would want to hear the good news.

The next day, when Mary Beth stepped off the elevator, the nurse at the nurse's station waved her over. "Angela has been asking for you, over and over again. I'm glad you are here."

Mary Beth hurried down the hall and knocked at the door. She opened it and found Angela in the middle of a therapy session. "Oh, sorry! I didn't mean to interrupt!" She started to back out of the room when Angela stopped her.

"Mary Beth, don't leave! I want you here," she said, grimacing as the therapist raised her right leg. She reached her hand out and beckoned Mary Beth over to the bed.

Mary Beth walked over and grabbed Angela's hand. Angela squeezed it tightly as the therapist continued to manipulate her joints. "This is the worst part," she said, through clenched teeth. Soon it was over and Angela was pulled to a sitting position, her legs dangling over the side of the bed.

Mary Beth helped the therapist put special socks on Angela's feet. They had neoprene puppy prints on the bottoms so that she wouldn't slip and fall as she walked. "We are going to stand you up, now," the woman said. She showed Mary Beth how to hold onto Angela's arm just below the arm pit and at the wrist. "One, two, three, stand!"

Angela wobbled a little, but stood still, looking like a soldier entering battle. Her brow was furrowed, and her mouth was a tight line. Her nostrils flared as she breathed quickly in and out.

"Do you think you could manage three steps toward the door?" her therapist asked.

Angela shook her head sharply.

"You can do it!" Mary Beth encouraged. "We'll help you. We won't let go for a second."

Angela looked at her feet, then at the door. She took a big breath and slowly moved her right foot forward.

The therapist nodded. "That's it! Good work. Now the other one."

It took Angela five minutes to take the three steps away from the bed. When the therapist tried to turn her around, she shook her head. "I want to go to the door," she said gruffly. Her eyes focused on the door handle like it was the finish line in a race. The three women inched across the floor. Each step was a tiny bit faster than the one before. After twenty minutes, they had made it the five feet across the room. The therapist held Angela up while Mary Beth hurried to grab the wheelchair on the opposite side of the room. They lowered her into the chair, and Angela let her breath out loudly. There was sweat on her brow and she was breathing hard.

"That was excellent!" the therapist praised. "I am so proud of you. Before you know it, you'll be doing that on your own."

They wheeled her back to the bed and helped her to get comfortable. The therapist promised to be back to see her soon and left the two friends alone.

"I am so proud of you!" Mary Beth gushed. She grabbed a washcloth and wet it with cold water. She handed it to Angela, who wiped the sweat off her face.

"I don't know what came over me," Angela confessed. "At first, I was afraid to try, but then something inside of me said just take a leap of faith, so I did. Then I got mad at this stupid bar and thought, 'The sooner I get walking, the sooner I can get rid of it.' Guess I have a stubborn streak."

"Whatever it takes," Mary Beth said. "I want to see you up and around, too."

The next day, Mary Beth returned to the hospital to help Angela with her therapy again. She expected to see that same fighting spirit Angela had displayed the day before. Instead, she was greeted by a sobbing mess lying in the bed. The therapist was trying to do her job, but Angela was refusing to cooperate.

"What's going on here?" Mary Beth asked, confused. "Angela, what's wrong? You had such a good day, yesterday. Did something happen?"

Angela sobbed even harder. The therapist said, "I'll come back later and we'll try again." She walked quickly out of the room and shut the door.

Mary Beth sat on the bed and smoothed Angela's hair back from her sweaty face. "What's going on?" she asked again.

"The doctor... he was here... I can't..." Angela cried.

Mary Beth tried again. "The doctor was here? What did he say? What can't you do?"

Angela shook her head and reached for the box of tissues by the bed. She blew her nose loudly and tried to calm down. "I... he... He said I have to be here at least another two weeks! I can't do this, Mary Beth. I can't stand to be in this little room anymore! He didn't seem impressed that I made it all the way to the door yesterday. I hurt so bad, but I can't roll over because of this stupid bar."

"I know this is hard to take, but your body is trying to heal from a major accident. You have to be patient," Mary Beth said. She managed to get Angela to take a few sips of ice water. Her color started to return to normal and she seemed less agitated.

"I'm never going to get to go home. What's the point of even trying anymore? Craig is gone, my business is probably caput, I don't have anything to live for now," Angela said, covering her face with her arm. "You might as well leave, too. You have a life, I don't."

Mary Beth shook her head. "Don't talk like that! You have lots to live for. Your mother has been coming as often as she can. We've all been taking turns minding your store, it's doing well. You are my maid of honor, too, remember? I'm not letting you off the hook for that."

Suddenly she stood up. "I have an idea. I'll be right back." She raced out of the room and down to the nurses' station.

She asked the charge nurse, "Do you think the doctor would allow me to wheel Angela down to the atrium? She is feeling very trapped, being in that same room all the time. Cabin fever, you know?"

"I don't think he would have any problem with that," she said. "I can understand the feeling. She's been cooped up here for such a long time. I think it would be good for her."

Mary Beth hurried back to Angela's room. "The nurse said that I can take you for a little trip in the wheelchair," she said, brightly. "Would you like to get out of this room for a while?"

"YES!" exclaimed Angela. The girls put the call light on and waited for someone to come and help them get Angela situated in the wheelchair. As soon as they got the all clear, they went down the hall to the elevator.

Angela beamed over her shoulder at Mary Beth. "I am so lucky to have you in my life. You always have a solution to my problems! Thank you for sticking by my side. I know I have been a pain today."

Mary Beth pretended to be put out. "You know, I'm keeping track of all of the favors you owe me. The list is getting quite extensive." Then she smiled and patted her friend on the shoulder. "I love you, you know that. I am happy to help."

Soon they reached the first floor and found the atrium. It was like a sunroom on steroids. Tall potted trees and low shrubs covered the floor. There were walking paths and benches hidden throughout the space. Small fountains gurgled and added to the tropical atmosphere. The girls wandered around and admired the flowers for a while, then found a secluded space where they could sit and listen to the water.

Mary Beth mused, "You know, a year ago it was YOU helping me put my life back together. I thought my world had come to an end with all those bad things that were happening to me. Then you came up with your brilliant 'Leap of Faith' plan and it saved me from my depression. Looking back, I wouldn't be where I am right now if it weren't for you. Thank you for being such a good friend."

Angela looked surprised. "I didn't do anything. You are the one who was strong through everything."

"Now it's your turn," Mary Beth decided. "Last year might have been my Leap of Faith Year, but this year is all yours. YOU need to take a leap of faith and decided to overcome these obstacles you are facing. You don't have to do it alone, but YOU have to be the one to take a leap." She smiled at her friend.

"Oh, take a leap, huh? Funny thing to say to a person in a wheelchair," Angela retorted. She hated to admit it, but Mary Beth was right. It was time to take her life back, one leap at a time. "Let's go find that therapist," she said. "I think I'm ready to try 'leaping' again."

Dear Reader,

I hope you enjoyed this book. The inspiration to write it came to me after having read the *Happiness Project* by Gretchen Rubin. Spending a year making changes to make yourself a happier person is such a great idea. I try to do this once a year by putting myself outside my comfort zone during the summer and trying something new. One year I bought a jigsaw and made wood projects. Another year I went to racing school and learned to autocross (a hobby that I share with my husband now).

If you liked *Leap of Faith*, head over to my website at www.missytarantino.com and check out the other books I've written. You can also join my newsletter from there, if you want behind the scenes information about my writing process, advance notice of upcoming books and other interesting tidbits. I tend to only send them out once a month, so I won't bombard your inbox!

On the next pages, you can have a sneak peek at another book I wrote called *free as a bird*.

It would mean a great deal to me if you would consider leaving an honest review of *Leap of* Faith on Amazon.

Happy reading!

Missy

Excerpt from

free as a bird

Chapter 1

It was a few minutes before the bell rang for school to start at Pine Elementary. Students were running around in the grass playing tag or throwing a football with their friends. The equipment was crawling with younger students. The swings were moving in their arcs. A constant flow of kids came down the slide. The teachers were relaxed, chatting with each other, cupping their hands around their coffee mugs.

Suddenly, a scream cut the air. For a moment, everyone froze. Students turned toward the sound. Startled teachers ran towards the jungle gym, where cries for help mixed with animal-like sounds of fury. A first-grader was sitting on the ground, holding his arm and rocking back and forth. Tears streamed down his face. He pointed up at the top of the metal structure.

The teachers followed his gesture and saw an older girl with stringy, dirty blonde hair crouching on the top bars. She was wearing a soiled green hoodie with yellow lettering on it that was at least three sizes too big for her. Her brown eyes looked wild in her small round face. Her teeth were bared. She looked a little like a scrawny bird of prey on its perch.

The bell rang and one of the teachers helped the young

boy to his feet and led him towards the nurse's office. Another teacher used her cell phone to call the office. "Tell Mr. Roberts that Destiny kicked another student on the playground. He needs to get out here right now. She won't come down off the jungle gym."

Soon the playground was deserted. Mr. Roberts arrived and the teacher followed her class inside. He pushed his black-framed glasses up on his nose and squinted up at Destiny. She stared back at him, not moving a muscle. Her knuckles were white from gripping so hard.

He slowly walked around the perimeter of the jungle gym with his hands in the pockets of his grey trousers. He counted his steps, looking at the tips of his shoes, not at her. When he had completed his circuit, he stopped and glanced up at her again. He'd been here before and knew better than to rush things. He brushed one hand through his thick black hair. He stretched his arms over his head to loosen the muscles in his broad shoulders.

Judging from the crouched position and wild eyes, that she wasn't ready to come down. No amount of cajoling, threatening or talking would bring her down when she was in this frame of mind. It was best to just wait it out. Let her calm down on her own. Give her some space.

He walked another circle around the equipment. On the

third trip, he noticed that she had shifted her weight and color was returning to her knuckles. Her eyes weren't as wide and her chest was not heaving like it had been. Body language was improving, but they weren't out of the woods yet. Two more trips later, Destiny slid to the ground and stood there with her hands in the big pocket across the front of her hoodie.

She wouldn't look at him, but she was calm. Mr. Roberts stopped walking and waited. Destiny was smart. She didn't need a lecture. She didn't need to hear how wrong it was to kick students. She didn't need him to ask what had happened. "He climbed my tower," she said in a gravelly voice. Mr. Roberts said nothing, just nodded. "He shouldn't have climbed my tower. I just want to be left alone." Her voice was quiet but forceful.

"Let's go inside and get you some breakfast," Mr. Roberts said. He glanced up at the sky. "Looks like it's going to be as hot as an oven today." Turning on his heel, he walked to the building. He pulled a wad of keys from his pocket and jingled them until he found the right one to open the side door.

They went to the cafeteria and gathered up some food. The trip to the office took a while. Every student they passed wanted to high five Mr. Roberts or tell him something. He made time for each one of them. When they finally made it to his office, he set her tray down and pulled a metal chair up to the corner of his desk.

The cherry wood shone in the light of the green lamp sitting on the corner.

As she ate, Destiny looked around. On the desk was a triangular piece of wood that said 'Carter Roberts, Principal'. By the door, there was a large black frame with several round medals artistically displayed around a picture of Mr. Roberts when he was State Wrestling Champion in high school.

Mr. Roberts busied himself at his computer, glancing Destiny's way every few minutes. As soon as he saw that she was finished eating, he turned to face her. He leaned forward and put his forearms on his thighs.

"You are as territorial as a wolf," he began. "Do you know what that means?"

Destiny shook her head.

"You don't want other kids on the equipment that you have claimed as your own. You think of the jungle gym as yours. Well, it's not. It belongs to all the students. They are allowed to play on it, just like you. I cannot allow you to hurt other kids here."

Destiny spent a long boring day sitting at a desk in the outer office that was way too small for her, doing work that was way too easy.

Chapter 2

The next day, Destiny managed to stay out of trouble through the morning recess time. When the bell rang, she pushed her way through the doors when they opened, not waiting to line up with her class, and was the first one into her classroom. Destiny's school had a lot of students who lived below the poverty line, and the school was given a government grant to provide free breakfast, as well as lunch to the students. Her teacher, Ms. Watts, had arranged the breakfast items on a rectangular table at the back of the room under a bulletin board that was made to look like an oval running track with lanes and starting blocks. The title said, "Ready, Set, Learn!"

Destiny stuffed two muffins and an apple into her pocket. Then she grabbed a juice, milk, an apple, and another muffin and walked through an obstacle course of desks to her own in the furthest corner of the room. She pushed some papers onto the floor and set the food in her hands on the grimy surface. She sat cross-legged on her chair and began eating. Papers stuck out of her desk at odd angles, torn and crumpled. Broken pencils and crayons littered the little tray in the front of the space inside.

She completely ignored the other students when Ms. Watts brought the class into the room. When she finished eating, she stuffed the wrappers into her desk. She pulled up the hood of her sweatshirt, pulling the cords tight and put her head down on the desk. Her eyes hurt and her head was throbbing.

Soon she felt a hand on her shoulder. Ms. Watts leaned close to her ear and said, "Destiny, are you OK?" It had been a rough night and she just wanted to be left alone. Now that she had food in her stomach, she was sleepy. Destiny chose to ignore the teacher and hope she would go away. Ms. Watts shook her short red hair and pressed her lips together.

"I'll come back in a few minutes to check on you," Ms. Watts murmured in her ear. She stood up and walked away. The place where Ms. Watts had touched Destiny's shoulder stayed warm for a few minutes. Destiny turned her face toward the wall and closed her eyes.

When Ms. Watts returned and again crouched next to Destiny, her hand gently rubbed Destiny's back. "Destiny. It's math time. I know you are good at math. Please come and join us." Destiny shook her head and writhed her shoulders to shake off Ms. Watts' hand. Ms. Watts persisted. Finally, Destiny looked up and saw her classmates staring at her.

"WHAT ARE YOU STARING AT, BOOGER EATERS??!!!" Destiny pushed with all her might and knocked her desk over. She stood up and stalked out of the room.

Ms. Watts followed her out and closed the door. "That was totally uncalled for, Destiny," she said, standing tall and crossing her arms. "You need to go back in there and clean up the mess and apologized to the class." Destiny balled her fists and punched the wall. She leaned against the wall and slid down. Wrapping her arms around her legs, she buried her face against her knees.

"Clean it up yourself, bitch," she mumbled. Ms. Watts clenched her fists and took a deep breath. Without a word, she turned on her heel and went back into the classroom.

A few minutes later, Destiny heard footsteps. They stopped right in front of her. Without looking, she knew it was Mr. Roberts. She gripped her legs harder and squeezed her eyes shut.

He was so annoying, the way he just stood there and waited. She had tried waiting him out in the past, but it never worked. "WHAT?" she said, looking up at him. "Go away and leave me alone."

Mr. Roberts squatted beside her on his heels. Destiny could smell his aftershave. It reminded her of pine trees. He calmly picked at some paint around his fingernails that he'd missed after working on his house the night before. He didn't say a word.

"God! You are so annoying!" Destiny turned her back to him.

Finally, Mr. Roberts gave a low whistle. "Wow, look at the time. It's like water rushing down a river. You can't stop it. Your class will be going to music soon. Do you want them to come out and see you here, or would you like to come with me to my office?"

Destiny took a second to weigh her options. Sighing, she stood and walked down the hall toward Mr. Roberts's office, head down and shoulders slumped.

She flopped into a chair in the corner of the outer office. She tugged her hood as close around her face as she could get it and leaned against the wall. She shut her eyes and fell asleep. Mr. Roberts let her stay there.

Chapter 3

The next day Destiny walked into the classroom to see that her desk was still on the floor, upside down, its contents still strewn about. She picked it up and shoved the contents back inside, not caring where they went. She went through her breakfast routine, shoving as much extra food into the pocket of her oversized green sweatshirt as she thought she could get away with. She kept her hood up over her head and her back to the class.

Instead of putting her head on her desk, she pulled a thick, stubby red pencil out of her pocket and drew pictures of animals on the back of the math paper Ms. Watts gave her.

When Ms. Watts came to check on her, Destiny tried to shove the paper into the desk. Not fooled, Ms. Watts reached inside and pulled the page out and straightened it. "These are wonderful drawings, Destiny. You are quite the artist. I'd like to see you finish the math on the other side first, then you can work on them. OK?" She flipped the paper over and pointed to the first problem.

"Fine," Destiny grumbled. She began working on the math

while Ms. Watts watched. It was multiplication. Destiny hated multiplication. She wrote some numbers on the paper, hoping the teacher would walk away.

Ms. Watts came down to her level. "Hold on a second, Destiny. Let me show you how to tackle this in a different way. I can see you are confusing the steps." She demonstrated the method the class was working on. Destiny sat back and crossed her arms. She didn't even look at the page.

"Now you try," Ms. Watts said, smiling warmly. Destiny picked up the pencil and wrote some more numbers.

"Not quite. Let me show you again," Ms. Watts said. She held out her hand for the pencil.

Destiny gripped the paper in both hands and ripped it in half. She screamed as she shredded it, "THIS IS STUPID. I HATE MATH AND I HATE YOU! JUST LEAVE ME ALONE!" She threw the pieces at Ms. Watts, slammed her chair backward and ran from the room.

She ran down the hall and out the doors. Once on the playground, she climbed up to her spot at the top of the jungle gym. Her eyes were wide and her breath was shallow. The wind blew her matted hair across her face.

Mr. Roberts came outside and looked around. Spotting

Destiny, he crossed the blacktop and stood at the base of the jungle gym. He put his hands on his hips and squinted up at her. A sigh escaped his lips as he pushed his glasses up his nose.

They went through the now familiar routine, Mr. Roberts waiting patiently for the anger to work its way out of her system, Destiny perching like a raptor looking for prey. When they finally made it back to his office, Mr. Roberts looked at this small child with dirt smudges on her cheeks, dark circles under her eyes, and shook his head. He glanced at the pictures of his family on his desk; his daughter's high school graduation, his son at the Special Olympics.

"Destiny, this is the third time this week you've been in my office for your behavior. It's like the bees returning to the hive, but there's no honey. What's up?" He spoke softly and calmly.

Destiny pulled her hood over her head and crossed her arms. She refused to look at him and sank lower into the chair.

Mr. Roberts changed tactics. He pulled open a drawer in his desk and pulled out a small plastic pumpkin. He pulled off the top and held it out to her. "Chocolate?"

She didn't move a muscle.

"You know, this chocolate is a lot like you," he said, unwrapping a piece and popping it into his mouth. Destiny closed her eyes and shifted her body away from him. "It comes in a wrapper that you have to peel open. But once you do, there's something sweet inside."

"Shut up," Destiny snarled. "I hate this place. I hate you. I wish you would just leave me alone." She pulled the hood further down to cover her eyes and pulled her knees up to her chest. She tucked her hands into her pocket. She found her stubby red pencil and rubbed it with her thumb.

Mr. Roberts put the lid back on the candy jar and slid the drawer closed. He let Destiny sit there quietly while he worked at his computer. Every once in a while, he looked at her out of the corner of his eye. Slowly she unwound her body and sat up. He continued to ignore her until he saw her feet touch the ground. "Ready to talk?" he asked.

She shrugged her shoulders and stared at the ground.

"Ms. Watts was helping you with your math," Mr. Roberts started. "She was showing you how to solve the problem and..." He paused.

Destiny rubbed her pencil some more. She shrugged her shoulders again and pushed her hair out of her eyes. Her toe traced the pattern on the rug under her chair. "It's too hard," she said. "I can't do it."

"And you didn't want to look dumb in class," Mr. Roberts said. Destiny nodded faintly. "Gotcha."

Mr. Roberts lifted a sheet of paper off his desk. "Ms. Watts gave me an extra copy of the math. How about we tackle it together, just you and me?"

Destiny looked at her fingernails and gave her signature shrug. "Whatever."

For the next ten minutes, she listened and watched as Mr. Roberts explained the math. He solved the first problem, then passed the pencil to her. Destiny wrote down the numbers as he explained the steps. By the time they reached the end of the page, she was solving most of the problems on her own.

They walked back to class together and showed the work to Ms. Watts. She smiled and praised Destiny's work.

"Sorry about what I said before," Destiny mumbled. She went over to her desk and picked up the shredded math paper.

The rest of the day she sat at her seat. She worked on her assignments. She continued to ignore the other students but managed to make it to the end of the day without any more outbursts.

When the bell rang the other students gathered their backpacks, lined up and said good-bye to Ms. Watts. When Ms.

Watts turned back to the classroom, she saw Destiny kneeling on the floor, surrounded by the contents of her desk.

"What are you doing?" Ms. Watts asked, confused. "The bell rang. It's time for you to go home."

Destiny didn't look up. She reached inside her desk and pulled out another handful of papers. "I need to clean my desk," she said.

Ms. Watts said, "This can wait until tomorrow, Destiny." She furrowed her brow. "I have a lot of work to do. You should get going."

"It will only take a minute," Destiny said, continuing to empty the contents onto the floor. Soon she was surrounded by the mess. She slowly put the textbooks back inside and then began taking small handfuls of old papers to the trash. Ms. Watts retreated to her desk and was grading papers. She watched Destiny make a show of organizing her belongings and straightening her desk and chair.

"Is there anything you want me to clean for you, Ms. Watts?" Destiny asked, walking up to Ms. Watts' desk. She had her hands in her pocket, rubbing her pencil.

Ms. Watts smiled and shook her head. She capped her pen and said, "No, Destiny, I'm fine. Thanks for asking. Now it's time for you to leave. I have a staff meeting to get to. Your family will be wondering where you are if you don't get going." She stood and walked with Destiny out of the classroom and down the hall.

As Ms. Watts watched Destiny walk through the big glass door, another teacher walked up. "I don't know why you are so nice to her. Not after the way she treats you."

Ms. Watts said, "You never know what someone is going through. She just needs to know that someone cares for her." She turned and headed to the office.

Did you enjoy the preview? Purchase *free as a bird* on Amazon!

Made in the USA
Coppell, TX
12 April 2023